FOUR O'CLOCK SIZZLE

Also by Joanne Pence

The Cook and Inspector Mysteries

DEATH ON A SILVER PLATTER

A QUICHE BEFORE DYING -THE MARINARA MURDERS

CLOSE ENCOUNTERS OF THE DEADLY KIND

DEATH BY DEVIL'S FOOD - BLIND DATE'S BITTER END

THE TAVERNA AFFAIR - THE MUSIC BOX MYSTERY

TRUFFLES TO DIE FOR - COOKING SPIRITS

ADD A PINCH OF MURDER - SALSA AND SECRETS

DEADLY EVER AFTER

The Rebecca Mayfield Mysteries

ONE O'CLOCK HUSTLE - TWO O'CLOCK HEIST

THREE O'CLOCK SÉANCE - FOUR O'CLOCK SIZZLE

FIVE O'CLOCK TWIST - SIX O'CLOCK SILENCE

SEVEN O'CLOCK TARGET - EIGHT O'CLOCK SPLIT

NINE O'CLOCK RETREAT - THE 13th SANTA (Novella)

The Donnelly Cabin Inn

IF I LOVED YOU - THIS CAN'T BE LOVE

SENTIMENTAL JOURNEY - A CERTAIN SMILE

TIME AFTER TIME

Others

SEEMS LIKE OLD TIMES - DANGEROUS JOURNEY

DANCE WITH A GUNFIGHTER - THE DRAGON'S LADY

THE GHOST OF SQUIRE HOUSE

FOUR O'CLOCK SIZZLE

THE REBECCA MAYFIELD MYSTERIES
BOOK 4

JOANNE PENCE

QUAIL HILL PUBLISHING

Quail Hill Publishing

Eagle, ID 83616

Visit our website at www.quailhillpublishing.net

First Quail Hill Publishing Print Book: June 2016

Second Quail Hill Publishing Print Book: August 2018

First Quail Hill Publishing E-book: June 2016

FOUR O'CLOCK SIZZLE

1

———————

San Francisco Fire Department Captain Warren Eisen, head of the Bureau of Fire Investigations, believed arson was the cause of the early morning blaze that gutted the storeroom of Easy Street Clothiers. It was an upscale store that catered to hip young men as well as older men hoping to appear "cool," and willing to pay a fortune for jeans, shirts, and jackets that looked well-worn when purchased. No three-piece suit, necktie or, God forbid, a bow tie would ever darken the racks of Easy Street.

If the cause of the fire was arson, the death of the man found in the store would very likely be ruled a homicide.

What Homicide Inspector Rebecca Mayfield found strange, however, was that when she and her partner Bill Sutter arrived at the scene, Easy Street Clothier's owner, Diego Bosque, had already gone. He put his store manager, Dan Peters, in charge. The detectives tried to locate Bosque, but he wasn't answering his phone, or heeding their voice message requests to return to the building.

No one, as yet, knew the identity of the victim. He was found curled on the floor of the storeroom as if asleep, an empty bottle of what is often called "Two Buck Chuck" next to him. He

was white, probably in his forties or fifties, thin and malnour-
ished. Judging from his clothes—definitely not Easy Street
quality—he appeared to be a derelict who had somehow gotten
inside with his wine and died of smoke inhalation while he
slept. Very likely, no one knew he was there when the fire
alarms went off.

After spending the morning talking to neighboring store
owners and others who worked nearby, and obtaining information on the employees, Rebecca returned to the Hall of Justice to
run some employee names through the system to see if any red
flags turned up. At the same time, Bill Sutter was doing what he
could to run down the name of the victim.

The Homicide Bureau was located on the Hall's fourth floor.
It consisted of a large, open main room crammed with inspectors' desks and filing cabinets, books, and computers. Off it were
interview rooms, and nearby was the office of the chief, Lt. James
Philip Eastwood.

As Rebecca entered the bureau, she was surprised to see
three of homicide's detectives, Bo Benson, Paavo Smith, and Luis
Calderon, huddled around the secretary's desk. Whatever Elizabeth Havlin was showing them was causing them to laugh like a
group of teenage boys pouring over their first copy of *Playboy*.
Rebecca headed their way.

"What's going on?" she asked.

"Oh!" Elizabeth cried. She shut the magazine they were
looking at and flipped it over, face-down. Rebecca caught a
glimpse of the cover: *San Francisco Beat*. It was a weekly pulp rag
filled with mostly scurrilous stories about the Bay Area's rich
and famous. Elizabeth's whole face turned bright red. "Look!"
she pointed to a vase of roses on a side table. "They just came for
you. Must be a secret admirer."

"For me?" Rebecca was surprised. The roses were beautiful.

The three detectives all but ran back to their desks. Rebecca glanced at them as she pulled out the note. *May these help brighten your Monday. —Richie.*

She smiled. How sweet! She couldn't even remember the last time anyone sent her flowers. And never at work. She wondered if speculation about her flowers was what the "boys" as she called the male detectives she worked with—and sometimes they did act like boys—had been chuckling over.

"Or, maybe they came from a not-so-secret admirer?" Elizabeth said with a knowing smile.

Rebecca's lips pursed. She didn't like the thought of anyone at work knowing about her private life. Especially not when it involved Richie Amalfi. It was bad enough that he was the cousin of the wife of her co-worker, Homicide Inspector Paavo Smith, but she always felt, sadly, that despite liking him a whole lot, that theirs was no "forever" relationship. They'd have a pleasant fling, but eventually each would go their separate ways. So she didn't want people she worked with to think more was going on here than actually was. "It's no one you know," she said curtly. Sometimes a white lie was better than truthfully saying, "It's none of your business."

"I see." Elizabeth gave a forced laugh.

Rebecca wondered why Elizabeth was acting so strangely, noticing she now had her arms crossed atop the magazine as if desperately trying to hide it.

"May I see?" Rebecca asked, holding out her hand. While most people would think they needed to "respect" Elizabeth's desire to hide the magazine, as a cop, Rebecca had learned to ask for and get what she wanted, when she wanted it.

"Oh, you don't want to look at it," Elizabeth said, nervously shaking her head. "It's a sleazy tabloid, that's all. Nothing but lies—gossip and lies. You can't believe a thing you read in it."

"I know that," Rebecca said. "It's why I never read it. But I'd like to be in on the joke."

Elizabeth drew in a deep breath. "Before I give it to you, I've got to explain. I had no idea what was in it. I only bought it for fun."

"Okay," Rebecca murmured, more puzzled than ever. And then like a beat cop who was tired of pussy-footing around, she said, "Hand it over."

Elizabeth handed over the magazine.

The cover screamed, *"San Francisco's Bad Boys: The City's 6 Most Enticing Bachelors."* On that cover was a montage of six good-looking men. And among them, smiling at the camera in a full, toothy grin, was the guy who had just gifted her with beautiful roses, Richie Amalfi himself. "Oh, shit!"

Rebecca usually made it a point not to swear because she'd grown so sick of the constant barrage of foul language she heard on the streets as a cop. But this time, she couldn't help herself.

"Don't ..." Elizabeth cleared her throat. "Don't bother to read it. It's garbage."

Rebecca flipped to the article. She actually was tempted to give the rag back to Elizabeth when her eye caught the name of another "bad boy." Diego Bosque, the hard-to-reach owner of Easy Street Clothiers.

Without saying a word, she took her roses and the magazine and headed to her desk. Watching her, the other detectives, Bo, Paavo, and Luis, looked ready to crawl under their own desks. One-by-one, each skedaddled out of the bureau. She was getting a very bad feeling about this. She sat down, stiffened her shoulders and began to read.

Our six bachelors aren't the Bay Area's richest men and not necessarily the most handsome. And yet, through force of personality combined with renown in their respective fields, everyone notices when one of these bad boys enters a room. And if you don't believe us, just listen to what the women—and a few men—who best know our six 'Enticing Bachelors' have to say.

The article went through the bachelors one by one—a boutique hotel owner, a tour boat operator, a restaurant owner, a software developer, and the two names Rebecca knew: an upscale men's clothier, and Richie. She scarcely glanced at the write-ups of the men she didn't recognize, but stopped at the write-up for Diego Bosque. Rebecca congratulated herself for allowing professional interest to trump personal curiosity ... for now.

It talked about his family moving to the U.S. from Argentina, and how he began his career by working in the men's department at Macy's in San Francisco. He quickly discovered an interest in fashion and materials. But then the article took a surprising swerve and implied that people on the wrong side of the law gave him the means to open a small downtown store that catered to young professionals, and that was why he now owned several satellite stores in the Cupertino-Silicon Valley area.

Bosque counted his fortune in seven figures. Also, he had been engaged several times, but never married. He even left one society debutante standing at the altar when he got cold feet—after her wealthy father had shelled out over a hundred grand on a big, fat white wedding with all the trimmings. Rebecca couldn't help but wonder if that wasn't motive for arson by the bride-to-be, her father, or both.

The rest of the write-up recounted, time after time, Bosque's role as a heart-breaker. She quickly scanned that and then turned to the section about Richie.

The article introduced him as a former real estate mogul turned entrepreneur and the owner of the city's hottest new nightclub, Big Caesar's, located near Fisherman's Wharf. Like Diego Bosque's biography, strong hints were made that the money he used to buy his first building wasn't clean. She actually knew where the money had come from, and she was stunned that the article didn't mention it. Only recently had

Richie told her about that side of his life. When a person had a problem, especially one with criminal or civil overtones, and needed it to "go away" or to be quietly handled, that person could go to Richie to have the situation "fixed." People paid big bucks for such clandestine assistance.

Strange, she thought, that the writer had missed that, but she was relieved he had. She didn't want the cops she worked with to know anything about Richie's income as a "fixer." He swore that everything he did was on the right side of the law, and although she believed him, she also saw first-hand that the line between right and wrong wavered quite a bit. And even if Richie wasn't doing anything illegal, the people he dealt with rarely had such scruples.

The article did say it was amazing that Richie seemed to know "everybody who's anybody" in the Bay Area. The writer also pointed out that he couldn't find anyone who would say anything negative about Richie. The article implied it wasn't because they genuinely liked him, but that something else was going on—something not quite "right." And, yes, the word was used again with all it implied: right versus wrong.

She didn't want to read anything more, but she couldn't help herself because the write-up next went to Richie's personal life.

Although no one spoke badly of him, the magazine didn't hesitate to describe him as the worst sort of Lothario. Two pictures were included of him with two of his former "lady friends." Both looked like models—tall, thin, and beautiful— one with long raven-colored hair, and the other with long, light brown hair streaked with blond highlights. Both, when interviewed, talked about him flooding them with flowers—Rebecca stopped reading, her eyes narrowing on the roses on the corner of her desk. He also gave them presents, wined and dined them lavishly, and was constantly attentive until they fell madly in love and believed he felt the same. Then he dumped them without so much as a goodbye, let alone any explanation. One of the women even shed tears as she relayed her story.

Rebecca's eyebrows rose at that.

What a bunch of horse ... pucky. The article was ridiculous. She'd gotten to know Richie well, and this write-up was completely unfair about him. He could be maddening at times, but that was no reason for him to be pilloried this way. There was a period in his life where he'd been in quite a tailspin and acted accordingly, but the reason for it was understandable. If anything, he should be congratulated for the way he, with the help of his closest friends, Shay and Vito, managed to pull himself out of that period and to move on with his life. But the author of the article didn't go into any of that. Instead, he just played up Richie's less-than-stellar reputation.

Over the past few months, every detective she worked with, plus her boss, Lt. Eastwood, had warned her against getting involved with him. She had visions of their reaction to the article, believing it, and most likely concluding that she was nothing but a pathetic, unsophisticated chump, a farm-girl from Idaho, naïve enough to fall for a charming, big-city wheeler-dealer.

The unfairness of it all made her sick to her stomach.

Visions of her weekend with him struck. They'd spent most of it together—Saturday night, Sunday, Sunday night. And it had been nice. Quite nice. They had even made plans for next weekend, hoping for a fun time away from the city.

She rubbed her forehead. The best thing would be if no one at work found out how close she and Richie had become. It'd be one thing if she thought they would stay together, but to tell the truth, she didn't know what to think about their future.

And now this. Doing a slow burn that was quickly growing into a major conflagration, she shut the magazine and turned it face down.

How could Richie not have told her about the article? He

had to have known about it. Did he really think she wouldn't find out? *San Francisco Beat* made *The National Inquirer* look like Pulitzer material, but people in the Bay Area read and talked about it. Its whole reason for being was to spread salacious lies that would get people to buy the magazine; they certainly didn't buy it to increase human knowledge or understanding. It was like catnip to anyone who liked Bay Area gossip.

Good God! She could imagine people lumping her in with the jilted, weepy women in the story. She could see it causing people, including her colleagues, to question her judgment. And her, a homicide inspector ...

Maybe she was just over-reacting. She opened to Richie's part of the article and read it again. The more she read, the more furious she became. If only she had a match—

"Rebecca? Hello-o-o!"

She looked up at the sound of Sutter's voice. "I didn't know you were such a fan," he said. "I'll be sure to get you a copy of *Hollywood Gazette* next time I see it. It's actually a lot better, the stories much juicier. Did you read the one about Elvis Presley being an alien?"

"Very funny." She turned to the page with Diego Bosque's photo and folded back the rest of the magazine. "Look. He's the reason I'm reading it."

"Interesting," Sutter said. "All this free publicity and Bosque's shop had to close due to arson. I wonder if he has a jealous competitor." He reached for the magazine and opened it so both pages were visible at once and then gawked at Richie's picture. "My, my. Look who's there. I'm sure the write-up about him is very uplifting."

"Are you standing there for a reason, Sutter?" she asked.

"The ME hasn't done the autopsy yet, but from all she's seen, it's almost certain the victim died of smoke inhalation. Which means whoever set the fire caused his death. So, I'm going to

Bosque's house, see if I spot anything there and to talk to his neighbors. His taking off right after a man is found dead in his store is more than a little suspicious, if you ask me. Want to come along?"

She shoved the magazine in her desk drawer. "Let's get out of here."

~

Richie Amalfi sometimes wondered why he still did what he did. As he walked through the house of his newest client, this was one of those times.

Logan Travis was not only a young, spoiled, hard-to-get-along-with Silicon Valley high-tech genius, but he was born rich which meant he never had to struggle a single day in his life. Not for money, not for brains, and given that he was a decent enough looking guy, not for companionship of any kind—male or female.

But now, Mr. Lucky was asking him for help. What kind of help, Richie didn't know yet.

He arrived at Travis's house earlier than usual because he'd gotten up earlier than usual ... all because his weekend was stranger than usual. Right now, for a variety of conflicting reasons, he didn't want to think about it.

The house was a boring little Craftsman on the edge of the Ingleside district, an area being gentrified into charming albeit small homes with price tags starting around a million dollars. Travis led Richie into the living room where a carafe of coffee waited. Two black suede loveseats faced each other in front of a sleek onyx fireplace. As each man sat, Travis poured the coffee.

He added sugar and cream to his, took a swallow, and then eased back in the seat. "I called you here to talk about my newest invention."

Richie nodded sagely even as his stomach sank. He knew next to nothing about computers and only hoped he didn't get hit with so much jargon he wouldn't have a clue what the hell Travis was talking about. Or get so bored he'd fall asleep.

"I've told you about the rather simple apps I've done in the past, but my newest invention goes beyond anything anyone has ever seen," Travis explained. "In fact, it's likely to blow up the way humans interact with each other. It'll be mind-bending. And worth billions."

"Pretty high expectations," Richie said, sipping his coffee.

"Look," Travis leaned toward him. "In your line of work, wouldn't you like to know who you can trust and who you can't?"

"In any line of work a person wants to know that," Richie admitted.

"Exactly!" Travis looked pleased. "And suppose you're dating, and you meet the woman of your dreams, don't you want to be sure you can trust her? That when she tells you she loves you, that it's you and not your money she's in love with?"

"Sure," Richie acknowledged. "What guy wouldn't? I mean, who among us can really understand women?"

With a Cheshire cat smile, Travis announced, "I've created an app that will tell you if a person is lying."

Richie put down his cup.

"I'm testing it now. There are still a few kinks, but I'll work them out."

"Really?" Richie asked.

"I cannot tell a lie," Travis said with a huge grin. "Not with my invention around. When it's on, it records every human you interact with. You only need to say the person's name so it can catalog who it is you're dealing with. It sends out waves that record pressure points involving any touching, from handshakes to kisses, and changes in voice patterns or tones. The more often you interact with that individual the more data it will collect. That way, it'll know when the person is acting out of character. Certain 'out of character' reactions are characteristics of lying."

"That's mind-blowing," Richie murmured, not too sure how much credence, if any, he gave to Travis' claims.

"Yes." Travis looked like a kid entering a theme park. "My app will tell you if someone who says they love you really means it; if a business client really can be trusted; if the house you want to buy really doesn't have any major issues; and so on."

Richie nodded. His job was dealing with people, and he couldn't help but imagine the trouble such an app could cause. More business for him.

"So, I have two requests of you," Travis continued. "The first is about my old partners, Mitch Voltz and Jason Singh. I don't want them to come back and demand a cut on what I've spent years developing. I want you to find out what they're up to."

"What makes you think they're plotting anything?"

"Because my security system tells me someone has been sneaking around my house and I can't think of anyone else it might be."

"In that case," Richie said, "why don't you use your app and ask them if they want a cut of your profits? You'll know if they're lying to you about it, right? Isn't that the point?"

Travis pursed his lips. "They know about the app and know how to circumvent it."

"More of those kinks, eh?" Richie said.

Travis stiffened and his cheeks reddened. "That brings me to my second request. People I deal with know about my invention. And most of them are easy to read, even without it. You, on the other hand, meet lots of people. I'd like you to put my app on your phone and see if it works for you."

"Are you joking? I don't think I'm your clientele."

"Wouldn't you like to know what people you talk to are really thinking? When they say something is wonderful, don't you want to know if they're telling the truth?"

Richie smirked. "I'm not sure."

Travis laughed. "Don't tell me you're scared?"

"Not at all." Richie wondered if the stupid app would have recorded that as a lie.

Travis stood. "Well then, I'll put it on your phone and show you how to use it. A little test run can't hurt, right?"

Richie had his doubts. He handed over his smart phone and followed Travis to a den filled with enough computer screens to rival NASA. Travis connected the phone to his computer, and then his fingers flew as he got into its settings and began the download. Richie frowned at what was being done to one of the great loves of his life.

"So, did you hear about the fire this morning?" Travis asked as he waited for his app to install.

"No," Richie said. "Where?"

"Easy Street Clothiers. You know that the owner's one of the—"

"Yeah, I know." Richie cut Travis off with a scowl. He didn't want to talk, or even think about what Travis was referring to. "Odd that the news didn't mention any fire."

"It was small. I only know because I've got a police band on my computer and get alerts if anything odd is going on in the city."

"I'm sure, then, that the fire means nothing," Richie said.

"Whatever, I still don't like it," Travis said. "Our connection to him makes me nervous. Ah! It's installed. I tell you, you're going to absolutely love using it!"

2

By the time evening came, Rebecca was glad to head for home.

Diego Bosque hadn't been at his condo. He lived on the top floor of an expensively renovated building on the east side of Telegraph Hill with a beautiful view of the bay. Talking to his neighbors had yielded nothing at all. None of them had seen him that day, and most had never even said hello to the man. They all claimed he kept strange hours and, while pleasant, wasn't very sociable. That wasn't at all what she expected after reading about him in the *San Francisco Beat* article. She wondered if the write-up on him was as biased as the one about Richie.

Rebecca and Sutter spent the rest of the day interviewing past and present employees of Easy Street Clothiers, none of whom—she had discovered after checking their names on the SFPD's database—had any criminal record. She had the impression whoever torched Easy Street didn't work there—unless it was Bosque himself. Or, perhaps, a very dissatisfied customer.

By the time she got home, she was exhausted, and had a raging headache. It hadn't been helped by seeing several clusters of people she knew at the Hall of Justice either suddenly stop talking or try not to look her way as she passed them in the hall. She was sure she was being paranoid. None of them knew anything about her private life, did they? And the magazine wasn't *that* popular. Or was it?

She unlocked the door to her small apartment, once a storage room off the back of the garage in a three-story building, located on a dead-end street called Mulford Alley. There were only two others living in the building. The landlord, Bradley Frick, lived on the top floor; and Kiki Nuñez, in the middle one. The best thing about Rebecca's apartment was that it faced the building's back yard giving her what amounted to her own secret garden.

She was glad to find a place where she could see at least a little greenery since she'd grown up surrounded by nature. Idaho had been a happy place for her until her father died and her mother sold the family farm. Soon after that, Rebecca learned the man she had planned to marry, the son of the owner of the adjacent farm, had apparently been more interested in holy matrimony to join their farms together than to join with her.

Broken-hearted, she'd moved to San Francisco, and eventually worked her way into a job she loved. Now, she couldn't imagine doing anything other than working homicide investigations, and seeing that justice was done. It made her feel that her work was worthwhile.

But right now, all she wanted to do was to crawl into bed and hope no one got killed in the middle of the night. As the homicide's on-call team this week, she and Sutter would be the first responders at any unnatural and unexpected death.

She opened the door to her apartment, and stopped, surprised. Richie was lounging on her sofa, his feet up, the TV on, with her little dog Spike on his lap. Her first reaction was happiness at seeing him, and she even allowed a small smile to form, but then she remembered the *SF Beat* article, and her good feelings evaporated. "Richie! I didn't see your car parked in the alley."

He smiled in greeting. "There was only one spot left when I came by, so I parked in a lot. I figured if I took it and you had to drive all around in circles looking for parking, you'd come in with guns-a-blazing."

She was about to deny it, then stopped herself. He was probably right.

"I was getting worried about you," he said, sitting up. "It's late. You work too hard."

She turned her back to him as she placed her handbag on a small table near the door, and her jacket on a hook that served as a coat rack. She normally gave him a hard time about walking into her place uninvited—although she had given him the key. He knew she didn't really mean it, that it was pro forma. But right now, she wasn't in the mood for any games.

She squared her shoulders and faced Richie with a frown. "Long hours happen when someone's been killed."

Her little dog Spike, a Chinese Crested Hairless-Chihuahua mix, had jumped off Richie and stood on his hind legs, his paws on her knee. She picked him up, hugged and petted him.

"Killed?" Richie cocked his head as he studied her, as if contrasting her warm greeting of Spike with her curt response to him.

She could all but see the wheels turning as he tried to figure out what was going on with her. It was easy enough to explain. She knew Spike would always be there for her; Richie, not so much. That was the reality that had consumed a lot of her thoughts that day. It wasn't what the article said about him—it was exaggerated nonsense. What bothered her was that it had caused her to think about their relationship, and not like the result. Professionally, going out with him was clearly a mistake according to her boss; emotionally, she was allowing herself to become far too involved; and logically, she knew that as time went on, the more their differences would matter—and those differences were a recipe for disaster.

The fact that the article bothered her as much as it did proved her point.

She didn't want to think about it and answered his question. "A homeless guy died in a fire. It seems he picked the wrong place to try to stay warm."

He used the remote to turn off the TV. "Was that the Easy Street Clothiers fire?"

"Yes. I'm surprised you heard. I was told the fire wasn't big enough, and the dead man not 'important' enough, to make the news."

"The whole thing is a shame," Richie said. "About the poor guy who died, and also because Diego had a good thing going with that place."

His words surprised her. "You know Diego Bosque?"

"Not well. I only met him a couple times." He took his phone out of his pocket, pushed a couple of buttons and said, "Rebecca."

"What?"

He glanced up at her, then at his phone. "Oh, uh, what caused the fire?"

"It looks like arson. We'll know more tomorrow."

"Arson? You're kidding."

"No." She moved to the center of the small room and continued to stand. "We've tried all day but haven't been able to get hold of Bosque. No one is able to reach him."

Richie frowned. "He's got more stores around Silicon Valley. If it's arson, maybe he went there to make sure all his stores aren't a target."

"We tried those locations," she said.

"Enough of all this work stuff," Richie said, standing. "I brought you some dinner. I figured you've probably only eaten vending machine junk all day."

She put Spike down. "I'm too tired to eat." The magazine again intruded on her thoughts. "But ... maybe you have some *news* for me?"

"News?" he asked. "No, not really."

Her lips pursed. "I see. Well, as I said, I'm tired and I've got a splitting headache. You should go home."

"Did anyone ever tell you that you get really cranky when you're tired?" He went over to the kitchen area—her apartment only had two rooms, a combined living-dining-kitchen and a bedroom. He took several takeout boxes with Chinese writing from the refrigerator, put some food from each box on a plate and microwaved it while he made her a cup of tea and opened a can of dog food for Spike.

"I really don't feel like eating." She followed him, and couldn't help but add, "Maybe I should just sit down and read a *magazine.*"

"I know. You're tired. You had a busy weekend, I guess," he said with a grin as he handed her the tea.

The last thing she wanted was to listen to him joke about their time together. "Don't you have to go to work, or something?"

"You know Big Caesar's isn't open on Monday nights."

"Maybe it should be," she muttered. But as the food heated, its spicy smell wafted enticingly around her. She had learned to love Chinese food after she moved to San Francisco. Her stomach growled. Richie grinned, which meant he had heard it. Damn. But she had to admit that he was right. She was starving.

He took the plate from the microwave and put it on her small dinette table.

"Aren't you eating?" she asked, taking a seat.

"I ate earlier." He leaned back against the kitchen counter.

She took a bite, and quickly another. The plate was empty before she knew it. Her headache was all but gone. Feeling a bit sheepish after the way she had talked to him, she said, "Thank you. You were right. I needed food."

He took a seat across from her. She saw that he had made himself a cup of tea as well.

Now that she was feeling a little more human, she took a moment to actually look at him instead of trying to ignore him. She had to admit she liked his looks and always felt a lift to her spirits when he was near. Her gaze drifted from his wavy black hair, to deep-set brown eyes, angular cheekbones, his nose, his mouth ...

She averted her gaze. It was better not to go there.

She sipped her tea. The man was a puzzle to her. Even after all they'd been through, she wondered why he took it upon himself to hang out with a cop. She knew from experience that hers was not the sort of job that attracted many men, and especially not a man with money, who owned a nightclub, and who acted as a "fixer" to some rather questionable people. She'd been well trained to analyze every nuance of everything said and done, and from that analysis to draw conclusions.

Such conclusions warned her to be wary. But as soon as she was around Richie, all her careful training flew right out the window. Especially when he did something as sweet as bringing her dinner after she'd had an exhausting day at work.

"And now you need some sleep," he said, even as he continued to look at her oddly, as if wondering why her behavior was so strange. "I know when you're 'on-call' you can be sent to a murder anytime of the day or night, and you need to rest when you can."

He did it again, saying the one thing that showed he understood her and her work; saying the sort of thing that would make her want to tell him to stay. And why shouldn't she?

To hell with his leading role in a gossip-laden tell-all. She knew him better than that. She was about to get up and put her arms around him when his phone buzzed.

He looked at it. "Odd. I'd better take this." As he listened, he stood. "I'll be right there," he said, quickly ending the call.

She stood as well. "What happened?"

His face was grim. "There's a fire down at Big Caesar's."

"Oh, no!" She followed him to the door.

"Get some sleep." He put on his jacket, gave her a quick kiss, and turned to open the door.

"Wait." She took hold of his arm. "I'm coming with you."

"No, you need—"

"I won't be able to sleep wondering what's happening." She picked up her jacket, handbag and gun. "Let's go."

Big Caesars, near Fisherman's Wharf, was a nightclub known for its big band, swing, and jazz live entertainment. The decor was elegant and its customers dressed accordingly. With white table-cloths, flowing champagne, plentiful appetizers, and a spacious dance floor, it was like entering into the type of fashionable supper club shown in films from the 1930's or '40's. Tourists were the first to discover it, and its popularity quickly spread.

As Richie's Porsche 911 neared the club, he saw fire trucks in the alley that ran behind it, an area with a loading zone as well as for garbage pickup. He pulled into a no-parking zzone and then he and Rebecca hurried to see what was going on. A lot of people had gathered to watch.

The club's manager, Tommy Ginnetti, stood at the entrance to the alley looking glum. He'd only been promoted from head waiter to manager a couple of weeks earlier when Richie decided the club ran well enough that he could hire someone to handle the day-to-day operations. Tommy was his guy.

"What's going on, Tommy?" Richie asked.

"I'm hoping it's not as bad as it looks," Tommy said. The words were hopeful, but his expression said otherwise. He glanced at Rebecca. "Inspector Mayfield. I'm surprised to see you."

"She's not here officially," Richie said, his mouth a firm line. "At least, not yet." As he looked at the smoke billowing out of the windows of Big Caesar's, he wanted to know exactly how this happened, and planned to question everyone he could. Logan Travis's "liar app" just might be useful after all. He took out his phone, tapped it a couple of times, and said, "Tommy."

"Yes?" Tommy asked.

Richie put the phone back in his pocket. "What happened, kitchen staff screw up? Somebody leave a burner on?"

"I'm sure it's nothing like that."

"How did you get here so fast?" Richie asked. He stuck his hands in his pockets. Despite the fire, the trucks, the people, the night was cold and foggy.

"I'm the one who called it in. I came by to see what's going on with the furnace. Last night, the club got a little chilly. When I was home today, I started thinking about it. Finally, I thought I should see when it was last serviced. I figured if there was a problem, we could get somebody here first thing in the morning so it'd be all set for Tuesday night when we open. I was in the basement with the furnace—and it does need to be serviced and the ducts cleaned out—when I heard a window break. I tell you, it scared me. I came upstairs to see what was going on, and saw smoke coming out of the storeroom. When I opened the door, the place went up in flames. I called the fire department, and then you. Luckily, they got here in a couple minutes."

"You heard a window break?" Rebecca asked.

"Yeah. I'm thinking the fire must have started in the store-room and got so hot it caused the glass to explode. I've heard that happens sometimes. I'm hoping the firemen put it out before it spread to the kitchen or offices. But it looks like they're dousing the whole place with water."

Rebecca took out her cell phone. She looked worried. Richie knew that wasn't a good sign. "What are you doing?" he asked.

"I'm calling Captain Eisen, the arson investigator on the Easy Street fire. He found, there, that an incendiary device had been tossed in through a broken window." She turned and started to walk away. "Warren, Rebecca Mayfield here. I'm at a fire and ..."

Richie stopped listening. What she was saying was troubling. Diego Bosque's shop was firebombed and now his nightclub. There was no connection between the two of them ... except for one thing ...

And didn't Logan Travis say someone was sneaking around his house?

No. No way.

He didn't want to think about it, and instead flung his arm over his new manager's shoulders as he said, "Thank God you decided to check out the heating system tonight. You saved the place."

Tommy looked pleased at the praise. "I hope so. We'll find out soon enough."

"He's coming," Rebecca said to Richie as she put her phone in her pocket. "It may be nothing more than a coincidence." She stopped talking and stared into the crowd. Her eyes narrowed.

Richie, too, looked over the crowd. She took a step forward, and a man, a stranger, seemed to notice her stare. He wore a San Francisco Giants' baseball cap and a beige zip-up jacket, and looked like a thirty-year-old suburbanite who had come to the city to take in a ball game.

Rebecca took another step towards him. The stranger backed up, cautiously at first as though testing the waters, not quite believing he'd been singled out. He bumped into other onlookers as he backed away, then looked over his shoulder, turned, and ran. She took out her badge and waved it over her head as she sprinted into the crowd. "Police!" she shouted. "Get out of the way!"

Richie was too dumbfounded to do anything for a moment and then ran after her. But almost immediately the spectators had closed ranks, and he didn't have a badge to clear a path. He caught up to Rebecca on the corner of Bay and Powell. She looked as if she was contemplating stepping into the intersection where four lanes of cars were zipping by, bumper-to-bumper. He grabbed her arm. "Forget it."

"Damn! The light changed as he ran across the street," Rebecca said. "And drivers here don't wait a second before they start to move."

"Who was he?"

"He was at this morning's fire. I wasn't sure until he ran. I'll run some checks on him. This area is lousy with security cameras. It should be easy to pull a photo of the guy."

Richie did all he could to neither show surprise or alarm at her words, but his mind raced. Why would both he and Diego Bosque have their businesses targeted by the nerdy guy he saw watching? The guy wasn't familiar in the least. He didn't like where this was going. "Okay," he said. "I'm heading back to talk to the fire crew. I need somebody to tell me how bad the damage is."

3

Rebecca spent the morning looking at security footage from the area around the Easy Street fire as well as the fire at Richie's place. As she'd suspected, the man with the Giants baseball cap was at both places, but he wore the brim so low she couldn't run him through any sort of facial recognition software. She'd tried last evening with no luck, and hoped to do better this morning. She didn't.

She then went to Easy Street Clothiers. The manager, Dan Peters, was a youthful fellow who epitomized the stylish look of the store in his loosely casual tan silk jacket, baby blue pullover and brown slacks. But at the moment, he looked overwhelmed and harried. Rebecca flashed her badge. "Hello again, Mr. Peters," she said.

"Call me Dan, please," he murmured, glancing at his buzzing phone and then silencing it.

"Is your boss here?"

"I'm afraid not." He swallowed hard.

"Have you heard from him since yesterday morning?"

Dan rubbed his temple. "He called late in the day and said

he still had some things he needed to handle, but he would try to get here. I never saw him, however."

"Did you tell him I've got to talk to him? He knows a man died here."

Dan looked even more distressed. "Yes, ma'am. He knows it."

She showed him the photo of the man in the baseball cap, but he didn't recognize the fellow at all.

She asked a few more questions, but he was of little help. She was about to leave when Fire Captain Eisen called.

The arson team identified kerosene as the accelerant used in both the Easy Street and Big Caesar fires.

The front doors of Big Caesar's were open wide as a crew worked to clean the carpets, scrub the tile and dance floor, and generally do all they could to remove any hint of smoke, water, and fire damage. A large sign posted on the front of the building said "Closed Tonight - Will Open Friday."

Richie surely hoped so. He decided to use the post-fire clean-up as an opportunity to scrub down everything in the club and shine it up the way a place as popular as Big Caesar's should be.

He guessed one good thing came from the arson attempt. He'd never realized just how much the nightclub had come to mean to him until he'd almost lost it.

The sound of hammers and the smell of fresh paint greeted him as he inspected the place.

It was going to feel odd to see the ballroom empty the next few nights. Usually the white cloth-covered tables were ringed with customers entertained by a band and singer. At least two bartenders worked, three on weekends, along with a number of attractive cocktail waitresses. The fresh paint on the walls would look good, however. Richie expected the reopening to be on-time and go well.

He spotted Tommy Ginnetti talking to men out back. He took out his phone, put on the liar application, and then said, "Tommy." He walked outside.

"Everything's under control, boss," Tommy said, "for the reopening tomorrow. Should be okay, but the band insisted they be paid even if we're closed."

"Yeah, well, I can see their point. I guess we're stuck," Richie said. He talked to the owner of the crew doing the restoration and clean-up. The man had found no serious problems, and Tommy's instructions to him were clear and precise.

Richie soon headed back to his office. He was glad none of the damage had reached it. When he took over the club, he had decided that if he was doomed to be stuck in an office, he wanted a nice one. He had a high quality walnut desk and book-cases put in, plus a plush leather desk chair. The office even had its own bathroom, with a shower. He didn't know why he'd ever need one, but since he'd had the private bathroom installed, why not? His desk, computer and such were on one side of the room, and on the opposite were a large sofa, a couple of side chairs, and a mini-bar.

He was tempted by the mini-bar as he looked at how high his paperwork had grown with this mess. He didn't trust anyone but himself to oversee the business's money, both incoming and outgoing, and forced himself to sit down and go over the invoices, recording each into his accounting program. Before long, his tie was off, and the long sleeves of his shirt rolled back to the elbows. He really hated this kind of tedious work.

He was staring at an invoice that made no sense and running his fingers through his hair when he was struck with the sense of being watched.

He looked up to see Rebecca standing in the doorway.

"I see that you're planning to reopen Friday," she said, walking towards him. He leaned back to enjoy the sight. She was tall—nearly his height—her body shapely in all the right places. Her hair was blond and straight, now pulled back in a pony tail for work. But it was her eyes that caused his heart to tango—big, blue, and expressive. He loved watching her walk his way, even when she was dressed in jeans, boots, and a black leather jacket—her work "uniform." He also loved that she had no idea how sexy she looked in it.

He smiled. "It's coming along, and we're even making some improvements."

"But you've also increased your security, right?"

"Of course."

"The damage wasn't as bad as you'd feared, I take it."

"We were damn lucky. And did you have any luck finding the guy you chased from here?" He got up and crossed the room towards the sofa and chairs.

She did the same and sat on the sofa. "Not yet. We caught him on security and traffic. He was the same guy seen at Easy Street Clothiers, but he kept the brim of the baseball cap too low to clearly see his face. Arsonists tend to enjoy watching their handiwork, which makes me suspect he's our man."

"I've heard that. Do you have time for a beer, or coffee?" He had a small refrigerator as well as an automatic espresso maker in the office.

"No, thanks. I'm on duty and can't stay. But I wanted to tell you that the accelerant used on Diego Bosque's store is the same as used here. So, what's the connection between you and Bosque?" she asked.

Why would she assume ... Surely, she can't have heard, he told himself. The story's not even out yet. Besides, she pays no attention to tabloids, and businesses don't get attacked because of them. "Who knows why arsonists pick their targets?"

Her gaze seemed filled with disappointment. "There is a connection between Diego Bosque, and you." Just then, her phone buzzed. "It's dispatch," she said, which meant she had to take the call.

She stood, her expression making it clear she wasn't happy with him. "I've got to go, but we're not finished with this conversation."

He sat down as he watched her leave without even a good-bye. He took out the liar app to find it had marked just about everything she said as a lie. What the hell did that mean?

4

———————

The crime scene was a six-foot long trash receptacle in a narrow, shade-filled alley in the Polk Gulch district, a middle-class neighborhood of mostly two- or three-story flats and apartment buildings. Also, a string of businesses lined Polk Street from the foot of Russian Hill to the foot of Nob Hill.

A young policewoman stood guarding the dumpster while other uniformed police kept a growing number of spectators away from the area. As Rebecca approached, she saw a black mylar bag on the street. When she got closer, she saw that next to it was fresh vomit.

A creepy feeling trickled along her spine as she showed her credentials and stated her name. Her partner, Bill Sutter, ran to catch up to her, and he also showed his badge.

The policewoman swallowed hard before saying, "Officer Meadows, Central Station."

"The victim is in the dumpster?" Rebecca asked.

Officer Meadows shook her head. "No."

"Where?"

She pointed at the bag.

Judging from the size, Rebecca's heart sank. "A baby?" she whispered.

Again, Meadows shook her head, and quietly stated, "We haven't found the rest of him yet."

The rest?

Sutter gestured that the bag was all Rebecca's. She snapped on her latex gloves. As her partner watched, she found the open end of the bag and pulled it wide. The smell of blood and death hit her hard, making her stomach clench so badly she stepped back, needing some fresh air. Inside the bag was a human head, but the way the head lay, all she could see was the top of it— thick, straight black hair, apparently so heavily gelled that even as the head was being removed from the body, the style stayed in place.

"Good God almighty," Sutter whispered.

Rebecca got down on one knee and carefully lowered the black sheeting off the head and to the ground, doing her best not to move or ruin any remaining trace evidence. She then tipped the head so that it lay face up. It was so bloodless, bloated and mottled, she couldn't be sure of anything, but at first glance, the features and skin color appeared to be that of an Asian male.

As Rebecca stood up, her limbs quivered from the horror before her. She took a moment and then focused on the police woman. "What have you got so far?"

The young woman drew in her breath, doing her best not to look down at the head. "The call came in about one this afternoon from the diner on the corner. The waitress, Marian Rohe, said a homeless man came by asking for coffee and toast, and saying he needed something because he was upset at finding a head in the dumpster in the alley. She asked the cook to take a look. He found the head and called us."

"Who took it out of the dumpster?" Rebecca asked.

"The homeless guy. He hoped he'd find something good in it. But the diner's cook is the one who, uh, messed up the crime scene."

Rebecca nodded. "Do you have the names of those people?"

"Not the homeless guy. He's gone. He took off when the waitress, Marian, said she wasn't giving away food no matter what he found."

Sutter chimed in. "I'll go talk to the waitress and the cook. I'll make sure we get his fingerprints so we can eliminate them from others on the bag. In fact, I think I'll do that right now. The crime scene unit should be here any minute." With that he practically ran out of the alley. Rebecca couldn't remember ever seeing him move so fast.

She surveyed the alley. It was one block long, running parallel to Polk Street, with entrances at both ends. On one side stood the backs of the shops, offices and restaurants that faced Polk, and on the opposite side were the backs of multi-unit residences that faced Larkin Street.

The first order of business would be to identify the victim. But how? She could go knocking on the many residential doors in the area, but it was hard to imagine something as violent as a beheading taking place in one of the residences, which were uniformly small with paper-thin walls. The businesses, especially after hours, seemed more likely as linking to a murder, but it was strange that no calls had come in, unless the actual scene of the crime was some distance away. But why leave the head here?

The dumpster was outside the back door of the third building. She knocked, but no one answered.

She walked around the corner to Polk Street to see what was on the business side of the alley. The third building was a large, well-known restaurant. She had first heard about it from Richie who told her that the restaurant, Kyoto Dreams, served some of the most exotic, most expensive food in the city. And that its chef-owner had a huge reputation.

She hadn't paid a lot of attention to the other bachelors in the article about Richie and Diego Bosque. But she was pretty sure one of them owned a Japanese restaurant.

She phoned Elizabeth in Homicide.

As the Medical Examiner's team took the victim—or what they had of him—to their lab, Rebecca's phone chimed. A copy of the article and the image she'd asked the secretary to send her had come in.

Rebecca looked at the photo of Shig Tanaka, one of the bachelors in the infamous article and the owner of Kyoto Dreams. She was all but certain she now knew the identity of the victim.

Rebecca entered another world. A reception area with delicate ikebana plants and intricate scrolls on the walls greeted the visitor of the Kyoto Dreams restaurant, and soft koto music played in the background. Instead of a large dining room with tables shoved close together, shoji-lined walls hid away small tatami rooms where people dined in intimate privacy.

A tiny woman in a kimono bowed deeply to Rebecca. "*Irasshaimasu.*"

Rebecca showed her badge and asked to speak to Shigekazu Tanaka.

"You are the police?" the woman asked in a hushed voice, her eyes wide and frightened.

"Yes."

"One moment, please." She used her entire hand, palm up,

to gesture toward some chairs, then hurried down the hallway as quickly as the narrow skirt of her kimono and her wooden getas would allow. In a short while, she returned.

"Please, this way. *Doozo.*" The woman bobbed up and down, speaking quietly.

At the end of the hall, the woman lightly knocked on a door, then opened it. "Hanemoto-san, your guest." She held the door for Rebecca to enter the office, then pulled it shut behind her.

Kazue Hanemoto gave a slight bow and introduced himself as the restaurant's manager. He was probably in his forties, short, trim, and wearing an expensive business suit. "I understand you have asked for Mr. Tanaka. He is not here at the moment. Perhaps I can help you."

"I'm afraid not. I need to speak to Mr. Tanaka," Rebecca said as she showed her badge and gave her name. "Can you reach him for me?"

Hanemoto looked nervous. "He is out of reach, I'm afraid."

"Is that common for him?" Rebecca asked. "Isn't he your chef?"

"We have other chefs."

"Is Mr. Tanaka all right?" Rebecca asked.

This time, Hanemoto didn't look at her, but stared at the ground. "We hope he is fine. For some reason, he failed to inform us of his whereabouts. We suspect he thought he had, but simply forgot."

"When did you last see him?" Rebecca asked.

"Last night. We expect he will be here to prepare dinner tonight."

"Did he stay until closing time last evening?"

"Yes, well, almost. A friend of his came, and the two left together."

"Do you know the friend's name?"

"Yes. Diego Bosque."

Rebecca drew in her breath. "Have you tried Mr. Tanaka's home? It's ... a matter of life and death."

Hanemoto stiffened at her words, then called in his secretary and asked her to call everyone she could think of to try to reach "Tanaka-san." At the same time, Rebecca got information about Tanaka's apartment and phoned his building manager, asking him to check to see if Tanaka was in his apartment but unable to answer his phone.

As she waited for the building manager to call back, Rebecca asked Hanemoto if he had known Mr. Tanaka very long.

"I can hardly remember a time when we weren't friends. We grew up just two houses from each other in Kyoto, Japan," Hanemoto said. "I was one year ahead of him in school. I went to the university and studied business, but Tanaka wanted to become a chef and went to a culinary academy. I thought he was crazy, but his fame grew quickly. Soon, he decided to open his own restaurant, and I became his business manager. The Kyoto restaurant did so well, we soon opened a larger one in Tokyo, and then in Honolulu, and finally this one in San Francisco."

As Hanemoto spoke, Rebecca thought about the *San Francisco Beat* article. Just as with Richie and Bosque, the implication had been made that Tanaka hadn't come by the money to start and expand his restaurants through legal means. "I would imagine it's rather expensive to start a restaurant," she said. "Did Mr. Tanaka's family have money to help him out?"

"Not at all. His parents are somewhat elderly, and they still live in Kyoto. They tried to help, but they don't have much. He needed to take out loans. That was where my expertise came in," Hanemoto said. "I made sure the terms were reasonable. But everyone who knew him was willing to help. We knew he would be successful."

"I'm sorry to ask, but are you aware of a not-so-flattering story about Mr. Tanaka in *San Francisco Beat*? The article made it sound as if some of the money he used was from questionable sources, and that he's a bit of a womanizer."

Hanemoto chuckled. "Of course all of us at the restaurant know about the article. It's pure rubbish. Everyone knows it's all lies, but Tanaka told us not to worry about it, that in San Francisco, that kind of story will make the restaurant more popular, not less so. I assure you, his loans were quite legitimate. Also, Tanaka-san does have a fiancée in Kyoto. He's very much in love with her, and they plan to marry soon. But, as he is often invited to events in this city and others, he needs a companion. The women who accompany him are friends. Nothing more. All of them know he's engaged."

Rebecca remembered how the tabloid had interviewed three women he'd dated in this country. The writer caught their reactions as he told each one that Shig had a fiancée back in Japan and showed them a photo of a delicate woman wearing a traditional kimono. Some of the things the jilted women said about Tanaka after learning he was engaged had made Rebecca's skin crawl.

But was it a reason for decapitation? She didn't think so. "Do you have the names of his closest female friends?"

He frowned at the request. "I shall ask my secretary to provide you with that information."

The phone sounded shrill in the quiet office. Hanemoto visibly jumped. His secretary answered and gave Rebecca the phone. It was the building manager. He said Tanaka's apartment was empty, and Tanaka's car wasn't in its space. The car was a brand new Mercedes S 550, with GPS.

Rebecca thanked the man and hung up.

Hanemoto stared at her. "I don't know what to say."

She had reached the point in interviews that she most hated, but it had to be done. "Mr. Hanemoto, there's something I need you to look at. Hopefully, it has nothing to do with your missing friend. But we must rule out that possibility before I go any further."

Hanemoto's shoulders sagged, and his gaze told her he had been expecting something like this. "I see," he whispered. "I'll do what I can to help."

5

———————

R ichie sat in his favorite booth at the very back of the Columbus Cafe in the city's North Beach district. It was an old place with dim lighting and high walls around each booth. Richie liked it and had gone there for years, from the time he lived nearby. North Beach had once been the Italian quarter of the city, and then became the home of the "beatniks" of the fifties and early sixties, and now survived mainly from tourists who enjoyed going to picturesque shops and restaurants that harkened back to both eras.

After the waitress took his order of a beer and a pastrami sandwich, Richie opened his phone to see what Logan Travis' new 'liar' application told him about Tommy Ginnetti. They worked together most of the day. The app had flashing red lights and yellow warnings marked throughout. But Richie trusted Tommy. Or, at least, he thought he should trust him. What was going on here?

He looked up as the waitress brought his food, and as he did, he saw his friend, Shay, enter the restaurant. Shay rarely ate out, so Richie had ordered without him. Now, he hit a couple of items on the phone, and said "Shay," and then put it in his pocket.

Shay, whose actual name was Henry Ian Tate III, was the person Richie worked with the most often outside of Big Caesar's, and he was also the most reliable. Although the two were close, there was a lot Shay kept hidden from everyone, including Richie. He was around Richie's age and few inches taller, but where Richie had dark hair and eyes, Shay's hair was pale blond and silky, and his eyes sky blue. He was also a skilled marksman and a computer whiz. His appearance, his style of dress, his mannerisms all made him seem like someone who'd just stepped from the pages of *Gentleman's Quarterly*. But when a person got to know him, he was pure *Soldier of Fortune*.

After meeting with Logan Travis the day before, Richie had contacted Shay to investigate Travis's former partners, Mitch Voltz and Jason Singh. Shay would understand what they were all about. When it came to technology, Richie didn't care how things worked; he only cared that they did.

Shay sat in the booth across from Richie and ordered tea. He waited until the waitress brought him a cup of Earl Grey and left again before he asked, "What's the story on the fire at Big Caesar's?"

"Not good," Richie said. He had fallen into ownership of Big Caesar's, taking it over when an investment didn't turn out the way he'd expected. To his surprise, he actually enjoyed owning it. Because of the nightclub, he even thought about giving up his other line of work—a business that relied on his know-how alone, with no building to manage, no full-time employees, and no need to hire performers. It was basically a safe and legal operation, although he had to admit that at times things went very wrong and could become more than a little dicey. And as a result, some people, such as Rebecca, didn't understand the business and told him he was crazy to keep doing it, legit or not.

There were some things a fixer can't fix, like Rebecca's unfavorable opinion of him being a fixer.

But last night, looking at the charred ruins of just one room of his nightclub, and realizing the entire building could have looked that ugly were it not for a fluke of good timing, he knew he would always keep *all* his options open. He'd been poor, dirt poor, and he now had money. He preferred life this way.

"It was definitely arson," he said in answer to Shay's question. "Yesterday, Diego Bosque's clothes shop was fire-bombed too. Not much physical damage, but some poor homeless guy sleeping inside was killed. Fortunately, no one died at Big Caesar's. But—here's what's worrying me—Rebecca said the accelerant that started the fire at Bosque's place was the same as used at Big Caesar's."

Shay's notoriously unexpressive face did show a slight narrowing of his eyes. "Diego Bosque. Isn't he another of the—"

"Yeah, he is." Richie took a long swallow of his beer. "I'm sure that has nothing to do with it. I mean, it's stupid. Silly. Whatever. Nobody the hell cares!"

"Okay," Shay said calmly. "I'm only trying to see what connection there might be between the two of you."

"None. I've only talked with him a couple times."

"What are you going to do about Big Caesar's?"

"Right now, the water from the fire trucks did more damage than the fire. I'm cleaning it up and found a couple guys to keep an eye on it round the clock until we can stop whatever's going on. I don't want whoever did this to come back for a second try."

"Can I help?"

"There's not enough info yet. I'll let you know. In the meantime, tell me about Logan Travis's fearsome duo."

"Wait a minute," Shay said, his eyes fierce. "Logan Travis is also—"

"I already told you, get off that shtick. It means nothing."

Richie could see from Shay's expression that he wasn't convinced, but Shay answered his question. "I talked to them both."

"Talked to them?" Richie asked. "I thought you'd just check on what they're up to."

"I did, and that's why I decided to see what they're like in person. They're working on a project I'm actually interested in. It's an app to compare train versus air travel. Nobody thinks about trains in this country, but some day, because of the way TSA causes delays and because of the goofy ways airlines come up with rates, trains are often faster and cheaper for short trips."

Richie was literally at a loss for words. Mr. High Tech was interested in trains? Richie shuddered at the thought of them. He even found the bullet train that California planned to run from "almost Sacramento" to "almost Los Angeles" incomprehensible. Who'd want to use it?

"Weird," Richie muttered, and watched Shay's lips slightly spread into what was, for Shay, a display of raucous amusement. "Okay, whatever, what did you find out about the two?"

"They aren't a problem. They have no interest in Logan Travis or his app. They say it's a crock. It won't work, won't ever work, and they call Travis a whack job. All that Travis will do with his app, if it were ever to go live, will be to ruin friendships and romances by having people put their faith in something that's erratic at best. Anything a person does outside their routine way of speaking or acting, it records as a potential lie. Someone once sneezed, and the app said he was lying."

Richie tried to remember if Tommy Ginnetti had sneezed or coughed as they talked to him.

"And another time, a guy told a joke, and the app said it was a lie. No, it was a joke."

"So the app has no sense of humor," Richie said sardonically.

"Even worse," Shay said. "Mitch told a story about an employee, a guy who had a secret crush on Logan Travis. Around Travis, he was always a bit flustered, a little tense, and he liked to touch Travis's arm or his hand to emphasize whatever he was saying. The stupid app thought he was lying, and Travis fired him. It's crazy. People's emotions are too complicated for an app to handle."

Good God! Could Tommy have a crush...? Richie shook his head; he really had to stop thinking about that dumb liar app. "So if someone is bothering Travis, it's not his ex-partners. You're sure of that?"

"Do you want to put Travis's app on your phone and see if I'm lying?" Shay asked, without a hint of a grin.

Richie blanched. "I don't think so."

"They also said Travis is a bit psycho. He's paranoid and because he spends so much time alone, he weaves little things into big ones. There were times, they both agreed, they were actually afraid of him. Maybe you shouldn't go back to see him. Just phone in your info."

"He's not scary," Richie said. "But he is nuts. I'll talk to him and try to convince him those guys are okay."

"The thing is," Shay continued, "if someone is lurking around Logan Travis's house, the question is who? And why? There's Diego Bosque's clothing store, your place, Travis's house—"

"I told you to get off that. It means nothing."

Shay took a sip of his tea. "By the way, *SF Beat* is already out."

Richie turned pale. "Already? I was told it's next week's issue."

"They always release them before the date that's printed. It helps them look more current."

Richie thought about the strange way Rebecca had been acting. Nah, she didn't read that junk. Impossible.

~

Rebecca was a hardened homicide detective, but even so, she found it difficult to watch Shig Tanaka's longtime friend and business partner, Kazue Hanemoto, doing his best to contain his emotions as he looked with sickened, unmasked horror at the head of his boss. The medical examiner, Dr. Evelyn Ramirez, and her staff had done all they could with the judicious use of sheets and other coverings, to make the head look not as gory as it might have. But still, it was clear that the body wasn't attached to it.

After Hanemoto left, Rebecca opened up the *SF Beat* article as she attempted to reach the other three bachelors. Although she had no definite proof the write-up was connected to the attacks, there was enough circumstantial evidence to warrant a call.

The first one she reached out to was Pierre Fontaine, owner of a boutique hotel near the top of Nob Hill, where wealthy customers had easy access to downtown shops and businesses, the Financial District, as well as the tourist attractions of China-town and Fisherman's Wharf. According to the tabloid, it wasn't unusual to find certain wealthy female customers, especially married ones, checking into the hotel for some very personal service from management. Sometimes, when she found herself shocked while reading something like that, Rebecca realized a part of her was still a country girl, despite the years she'd worked in the notoriously avant garde city.

Fontaine was in Los Angeles at the moment. His secretary took a message.

She then tried to reach Logan Travis, a software engineer who designed one lucrative application after the other, mainly for smart phones. He would sell the app to the highest bidder, which was often Apple, and then develop an equally lucrative new app. His problem, according to the article, was that he was always working. Even when not physically at his office or even his desk, his mind was always on the job. He'd make a date and then forget to show up for it; sometimes, he'd even forget while with his date and walk out of a restaurant or theater without him (the article made it clear he only dated men) and without paying. And then he wouldn't apologize or even offer to pay back the money spent. His dates were left not knowing if they had done something wrong, or were simply so boring he ditched them. Whichever it was, the tabloid was able to find plenty of men who still held a grudge because of the way they'd been treated. They swore they would never forgive him.

She couldn't get through to him or to anyone at the number listed for his company. She left voice messages.

Last was Moss Brannigan, owner and operator of the biggest tour boat on San Francisco Bay. He had ginger-colored hair, a bushy beard, sparkling blue eyes, and in every picture he wore a replica of a commander's navy blue jacket plus a matching cap with a shiny black brim. He was definitely a woman-in-every-port type of guy—several of whom he had married and then either divorced or abandoned. According to the article, he had never legally divorced his first wife. The write-up also implied his business was in a financially precarious state.

She ended up leaving a message with his tour boat operators for him to call her.

Rebecca pushed aside the magazine after making the calls, and she could only shake her head at the litany of sleazy dealings and hurtful relationships the article had exposed. She couldn't help but wonder how much of all she'd read was actually true, and if true, instead of appalled or disgusted, the write-up only made her feel sad.

Earlier, Rebecca had requested a Japanese interpreter to help her out, asking that he arrive after 5:00 that afternoon, which would be 8:00 the next morning in Japan. When the young patrolman from the Taraval station arrived, she briefed him on Shig Tanaka's murder, and had him call the Kyoto police department. She was put through to a homicide detective named Sugiwara, who fortunately spoke excellent English.

She explained to Detective Sugiwara what had happened. He asked a number of questions and eventually said that he would have to go to Tanaka's parents with the news. He said he must tell them face-to-face, especially because of the beheading, which he suspected would be impossible to suppress. Rebecca agreed and understood. The detective also promised to go to Tanaka's Kyoto restaurant to see if anyone knew anything at all. "But there is one thing you should know," Sugiwara said.

"Yes?"

"Two years ago, the Kyoto police did an investigation of racketeering by the Yakuza. Do you know that name? I believe you call them 'Japanese Mafia.' Tanaka was part of that investigation."

"You thought he was part of the Yakuza?" Rebecca asked.

"We weren't sure because there were rumors ... but then, there are always such rumors. Tanaka was cleared, however. It was found that Tanaka's benefactors might have had some small association with the Yakuza, but nothing illegal was shown."

"I see," Rebecca said, noticing how nuanced the detectives words were.

"I suspect," Sugiwara added, "whatever had caused Tanaka to be killed has its roots in San Francisco, but if I find anything here that might help, I will contact you immediately."

Rebecca thanked him for his help. She then decided to go to the apartment of a woman Hanemoto had told her about, Tanaka's "lady friend" of the longest duration, Michiko Yamata. Michiko was home, but she was too broken up to be of any help. Although she said she knew about Tanaka's engagement to "a woman in Japan who was a stranger to him," it was clear to Rebecca that Michiko was in love with the chef and had hopes of a wedding in their future.

Not long after, Rebecca got word that Tanaka's car had been located. It wasn't because of his pricey GPS system, but because the car had been towed by the city for having been parked too long on Grant Avenue near Broadway. It was an area of bars and strip joints—an area Tanaka enjoyed going to now and then after his restaurant closed.

She sent the crime scene unit to retrieve the car. So far, their analysis of the dumpster and street where Tanaka's head had been found gave her no useful information at all. She hoped the car would be different.

She was gathering lots of information about Tanaka, but nothing that gave any clue as to why he would have been killed. Also, he was last seen with Diego Bosque, who was still missing.

She could think of one person who knew both men and just might have some answers for her. This time, she intended to get them.

She phoned Richie.

6

Rebecca and Richie agreed to meet at a small steakhouse near Castro—a halfway point between his house and her job. She might be working a murder investigation, plus the death in the arson fire, but she needed to eat dinner, and could justify having company while she did so.

The restaurant looked much like a European bistro, with exposed wooden beams, red and white checkered tablecloths, and a dark, round, wax-covered bottle holding a lit candle on each table. Richie was already at a table when she arrived. He had a bottle of red wine and two glasses in front of him.

She sat across from him. Without any preliminary words of greeting, she said, "This is very serious."

He reached for her hand and with a grin said, "You and I? I didn't realize how much you cared."

She pulled her hand back. "It's about my latest crime scene."

The way her voice turned soft, the way she looked both worried and sad, caused him concern. "What is it?"

She drew in her breath. "Shig Tanaka has been murdered."

A cold chill rippled down his backbone. All he could do was look away.

"I remember you telling me about his restaurant," she said. "About us going there one of these days if I could face the idea of raw octopus tentacles." She put her hand over his. "I'm sorry to have to tell you about your friend. And I'm also worried about you—the arson fires, and now this. You knew both men involved."

"Yes," he whispered.

She waited, looking at him as if she expected him to say something. "I liked Shig," he murmured. "We never hung out much together, but we did play a few rounds of golf." Here he'd been upset about a little fire and worried about paint jobs and invoices, and all the while a friend had been killed. A friend who was a part of …

Could that be what she was waiting for him to tell her? He studied her.

Damn! She knows.

He poured her some wine. "So you've read the article, and knowing you, probably more than once."

"Yes." Her voice was calm. "I have."

"It's a tabloid, Rebecca. You know what they're like."

She spoke slowly and carefully. "I know, and the only reason I care at all about the article is because, now, one 'enticing bachelor' is dead, another is missing, and there have been two arson fires. They've got to be connected, somehow, to the write-up." She folded her hands.

Just then the waitress came by to take their orders. Richie waited until she was gone before he leaned towards Rebecca across the table. He didn't need Travis's liar app to know, despite her words, the article had her steamed. "It's just a dumb article filled with exaggeration and innuendo. There's no reason for it to lead to anything, let alone arson and murder. There's got to be another explanation."

"What other explanation?"

"I don't know. Tell me about Shig. Was he killed at work, or what? Did it look like a robbery or something?"

She shook her head. "That's the problem. We don't yet know where he was killed. No crime scene, just the spot where we found ... him."

He looked at her quizzically. "But it wasn't where he died? Is that what you're saying?"

She bit her bottom lip, which meant she was truly bothered by all this. "Don't say anything until it's reported, but too many people know to keep it a secret much longer. He was beheaded."

He froze. That was the last thing he ever expected to hear. His mind raced. "Do you think it was some sort of terrorist attack?"

"No." She took a good-sized swallow of the wine. "The M.E. concluded that he was dead before his head was removed, thankfully. And wherever it happened wasn't near the spot where the head was left because a massive amount of blood is lost in such a situation."

He placed his hand on hers and rubbed it gently, compassionately. "I'm sorry you have to deal with something so ugly."

"All murders are ugly," she said, again removing her hand from his touch. "But I'll be quite glad to find whoever it was and get that bastard off the streets."

"I know you will," he said.

She swallowed hard. "The rest of his body is still missing."

Richie made no comment; he couldn't imagine something so macabre.

"We understand he's only about five-foot nine, but weighed well over two-hundred fifty pounds. That's a lot to keep hidden," she said.

Richie took a deep breath and slowly let it out, trying to

come to grips with all he was hearing. "He was one of those guys who gained weight easily, and then would go on a starvation diet to take it off." He tried, but failed, to joke. "A chef's curse, I'd say."

"So I've gathered from photos I've seen," she said.

"Maybe someone didn't want to deal with moving all that weight, so just left the head for identification," Richie suggested.

Rebecca frowned. "Most murderers aren't that finicky, or so interested in providing identification. It's got to be something else—a message, most likely, for the police or someone else."

He nodded thoughtfully.

The waitress brought their steak dinners out to them.

Rebecca picked up her knife and fork, but then put them down again. She could scarcely keep the irritation out of her voice as she said, "I don't understand why you didn't at least mention the *San Francisco Beat* article to me."

Richie didn't care for her tone and took a sip of his wine before answering. Rebecca buttered her dinner roll, glaring at him and waiting. Finally, he said, "Maybe I was hoping you wouldn't see it."

"But you knew the article was out there. You knew you and Bosque were in it, and both of you had your places firebombed. Two plus two, Richie!" The more she spoke, the angrier she became. "How could you not say anything?"

He hated being pushed by anyone, and his irritation quickly matched hers. "What, I'm supposed to think some crazy person is out there who hates bachelors? Or some guy who's jealous of us? Or maybe it was done by some woman who was jilted, read the article, went nuts and decided to take out her bitterness on all of us in the story?"

He could see her working to maintain her cool. "Whatever the cause, you could see that something is going on with the bachelors in the write-up."

Damn! "Can't you see you're jumping to conclusions?"

She lost it. "I'm jumping to common sense! Something that seems in short supply around here."

It was his turn to fume. "There could be other reasons for what's going on."

"Name one."

He leaned back, arms folded. "Diego and Shig seemed to have some sort of business dealings with each other."

That set her back. "They did? I haven't come across a hint of anything to confirm that."

"I just confirmed it for you."

"How do you know?" she asked, her eyes narrowing.

He gripped the edge of the table. "You ask for my help and when I give it to you, you're suspicious?"

"No, I'm not!"

He frowned. "You're still mad about that stupid tabloid."

"Of course not! I couldn't care less." Her back stiffened. "And anyone who knows you was hardly surprised by what it said!"

"Gee, thanks. That's really great, Rebecca. Now I know what you honestly think of me." He stood, took out a roll of money, peeled off enough to cover both dinners, and dropped it on the table. "Give Spike my steak. He'll enjoy it more than I will."

"Wait," she said. "You can't just—"

"Oh no? Watch me."

"Stop! You haven't told me about the other bachelors yet! And I don't want you to pay for my dinner!"

He had no idea what she did next, because by the time she finished giving him orders, he was already out the door.

Richie decided to take Shay's advice and not go back to Logan Travis's home. Instead he asked for a meeting at a bar owned by an old friend of his, Johnny Fazano. For one thing, he needed a stiff drink to calm him down after his fury at Rebecca. He really didn't need her nitpicking his every move, always ready to criticize. One of these days, one happy day, he was going to meet someone who'd make him forget all about that cranky, uptight, suspicious cop. And then he'd never look back.

What was unfortunate was that he had had glimpses of another side of her—a side he really liked. A lot. When she wasn't going all 'Rebecca Rulebook' and hard-ass cop and every other walking cliché there was to prove that she was every bit as tough as any male cop, she could be warm and funny and fun to be around.

In fact, when he thought about her, about the way she handled herself, did her job, pulled herself up in the ranks of what was still very much a "man's world," he admired her. A lot.

From the time he first met her on Christmas Eve when he went to homicide looking for help from his cousin's husband but found Rebecca instead, he kept trying to walk away, and to stay away, from her. It hadn't worked. Until now.

Now, he'd had it.

Sometimes he wished he'd never moved their relationship along to the next level. But at the same time, he found her too damned irresistible to keep walking away from. After they'd solved a case together—a case that had put his own mother in jeopardy—he knew it was decision time. He couldn't get her out of his mind. Whatever was going on between them had clearly driven him mad.

His thoughts returned to a Saturday night not long ago, and how, after he had closed up Big Caesar's, he realized he couldn't take what was going on between them any longer. He needed her, and more than anything physical between them, he wanted to know if she felt the same way about him. If not, he vowed he would never see her again.

He had been heading home, but turned towards Rebecca's apartment instead. Then, like some dummy, he'd stood out in the rain and phoned her.

He'd been about 50% sure she'd hang up on him when he told her he was outside her apartment. Instead, she opened the door.

He'd been a good 60% sure she wouldn't let him whisk her out of her apartment to his car. She went with him.

Some 70% sure she'd balk at going into his house. She didn't complain.

Definitely 80% sure she'd demand to be taken back home when he put his arms around her. She moved closer.

And 90% sure she'd never welcome anything more than a chaste kiss. Instead, she made it 100% clear she was feeling exactly the way he was, and wanted the same thing.

He wouldn't have been surprised if she had walked out while he slept that night, but she hadn't, and they had had such a good time together on Sunday, it still boggled his mind. They mainly stayed at his place, except for going out for lunch and taking a long walk along Ocean beach in the afternoon. For dinner, they ordered a pizza and put a baseball game on the TV. He scarcely watched the game, so busy was he watching Rebecca.

Everything had been so perfect it actually scared him. He hadn't felt that way being with a woman since ... well, not for a few years. And now ...

What a romantic idiot he'd been. If that was all it took to destroy her faith in him, the hell with her.

He downed his whiskey and asked for another. That stupid tabloid had sent all his hopes about her straight down the crapper.

They'd spent the next weekend together, and the next. How could she have changed that much from Monday morning when she left his home, his bed, to return to her apartment to get ready for work, to tonight? She was loyal to a fault.

And that, he realized, was the problem.

The article had depicted him as anything but loyal. A guy who got women to fall in love with him only to dump them. One who sent flowers .... His hand went to his forehead. The roses. He had sent them thinking they might make her happy, let her realize how much she was on his mind.

It had been a perfect storm of bad timing. And now that he'd walked away, he should simply say good riddance.

He still was trying to convince himself that the "good riddance" sentiment was right and just, when Travis finally arrived.

Richie took one look at him and decided Shay had been right in his warnings. Travis came into the bar wearing a red wig that made him look positively crazy. All he needed was clown face make-up and a red ball for his nose and he could get a job with Ringling Brothers. As soon as Richie saw him, he took his drink—Jack Daniels on the rocks—and moved from the bar to a dark table in the back of the room.

The bartender gave him a "What the hell?" look. Richie rolled his eyes. He knew Johnny always looked out for him and would keep a close watch on Logan Travis.

Richie quickly told Travis the results of Shay's investigation of his former partners, Jason Singh and Mitch Voltz, leaving out the part where the two men thought Travis was crazy and his design badly flawed. Travis looked neither happy nor upset to hear there was no indication his former partners, or anyone else, wanted to kill him.

"Maybe it's not Jason or Mitch who's trying to kill me," Travis said. "But somebody is. I know it. Somebody killed Shig Tanaka, and I heard Bosque is missing. I bet he's dead, too. I was in that magazine article, and so were you."

"Nobody was killed because of a magazine article," Richie said.

"It could have been a former lover pissed off at him," Travis said. "Thank God I don't have any of those. Not women, at least. And men are much more rational and understanding about such things."

Richie just nodded. Wasn't that the truth!

"I heard from a good source," Travis added, his voice low, "that Tanaka was beheaded. Women don't do things like that."

Richie sipped his whiskey. "True."

"Why was he killed?"

A cocktail waitress came by, but Travis waved her off.

"Whatever the reason, I'm sure it has nothing to do with you. You should go back home and stop worrying," Richie said.

"I don't know about that, but before I go anywhere, I need to know how my app is working for you. Do you like it? Have you used it much?"

Is there no ridding me of this weirdo? "I don't know. I used it a couple of times."

"Let's see," Travis said as he took the phone.

"Who's this Tommy?" Travis asked. "He lies to you all the time."

Richie swallowed. "He's my new manager. I wonder if I shouldn't have given him so much responsibility?"

"I don't know, but there's something going on with him." Travis's words were dire.

"What about Rebecca?" Richie asked.

"Whoa. Tense. Lies. I think she hates you."

"Great. That's just what I want to hear," Richie muttered.

"But this last one ... Hmm. Looks like there's a problem with my app," Travis said.

"What do you mean?"

"This guy, Shay. Obviously, the two of you talked, but the app recorded no reactions from him at all. No positive, no negative. Not a blip. I've never seen this before. Got to be something wrong. I'll have to figure out what and work on it."

"Good," Richie said with an inner chuckle. He always knew Shay had ice in his veins. "You do that."

"Anyway, I'm leaving," Travis said. "Would you hire a security team for me? I want more than computers protecting me. All this trouble because of a sleazy magazine article has me feeling paranoid."

"No kidding," Richie said as he went back to stewing over which part of Rebecca's conversation to him had been a lie. Or, was all of it? Then he realized Travis was still staring at him. "Okay, I'll find a security crew for you. And after that, I'd say our business is finished."

"Maybe," Travis said and then he sauntered out of the bar.

"Good riddance," Richie murmured. He slowly finished his drink. It hadn't helped. He thought about ordering another, but decided the best thing to do was to go home.

The hell with all of them, he thought, as he went to the bar and put some money on it to pay for his drinks. He then turned around ... to come face-to-face with two young, skinny, Latino-looking thugs.

"Richie?" The "spokesman" had long black hair and a thin, wispy mustache so long it reached to his even stringier-looking goatee.

Richie nodded.

"Good. Outside."

Richie almost said, "No," when he saw the flash of a steel blade in the man's hand.

Richie glanced at Johnny and gave a small shake of the head.

Next thing, Johnny aimed a shotgun at the two punks. "I'd say it's time for you fellas to leave."

The few other bar patrons saw the firearm and ran for the exits.

The thugs eyed each other.

"Right now," Richie said, "the people who left are calling the cops. I think you've got about ninety seconds, max."

Without another word, they left.

Richie faced the bartender and sat back down on a stool. "I think I'll have another drink after all."

7

Rebecca left her desk the next morning to walk to the *San Francisco Beat* magazine office. For once, the sky wasn't gray and foggy, but bright with sun. The tabloid's office wasn't far from the Hall of Justice. Sometimes it was easier to walk than to fight traffic and then hunt for parking.

It was strange, Rebecca thought, as she walked, how quickly things could change in life. She'd thought her life might be moving in one direction, and then, at the drop of a hat—or a magazine article—it had made a complete U-turn. She hadn't thought, until she faced Richie at the steakhouse, how deep the sting of the *San Francisco Beat* article had hit. And then, out of her mouth, came words that were both hateful and unfair. As soon as she'd said them, she regretted it, but was too angry to say so.

Well, it was probably for the best. This way, they could end it now, before things became even more complicated between them.

But now, she had work to do and the magazine article was, so far, the only solid connection she had between the two arsons and Tanaka's death. And that was the reason for her morning stroll.

The address she sought was in an old building on the ground floor, right behind a tattoo parlor. She knocked and then pushed open the door.

She entered a large open space with two women working at a table in the back of the room, and a third sitting at a computer near the door. The woman at the computer glanced up. "Yes?"

Rebecca explained who she was and that she would like to speak to the editor.

She had hardly finished when a tall, thin Chinese woman, probably in her forties or so, left the back table and approached her. "I'm the editor," she said. "Plus the owner, manager, and chief writer. Liv Wong." She held out her hand.

They shook, and then Rebecca explained why she was there. Liv Wong had heard of the arsons and the deaths, and she was concerned, but she found it far-fetched to imagine her article had anything to do with them.

"The article has a by-line, Connor Gray," Rebecca said. "Does he work here?"

"No. He's a free-lancer, as are all our writers except me. When I heard of the story idea, I decided to run with it. I'd used Connor before on an investigative piece and called him. He jumped on it."

"Where did you get the photographs used? And where did you find out the names of former girlfriends and boyfriends to interview?"

"Connor handled everything. My only requirement was that the story be current, not about scandals from years ago."

"So your involvement was ...?" Rebecca asked.

"To okay the story, have my lawyer go over it for anything we might be sued over, decide on which photos to use, and to do big-picture editing. I want my stories to be quick, exciting, and controversial reads."

"Have you had this job very long?" Rebecca asked.

"Four years. I bought the magazine when it was struggling. I hoped to make it more hip, and very San Francisco. I think I've succeeded. We'll see what this issue brings. So far, we've had so many calls for extra copies, we actually did a reprint."

"Does that happen often?"

"Never. Although I must say the arson fires may have sparked that interest. To our surprise, in their news report, the *Chronicle* mentioned that the owners of the two businesses involved were subjects in this week's *SF Beat*. They even gave the title of the article."

"I suspect you've had prior jobs with magazines?"

"I did. My last job was with *Sunset Magazine*. I left when I was pregnant with my second child. That was a few years ago. My two girls are now in seventh and fourth grades, so I've come back to work, re-establishing old contacts and such."

"Nice," Rebecca said.

"Yes, it is."

"May I have the address and phone number of the writer?"

"I've got a phone number." She pulled out her phone and found the number and texted it to Rebecca's phone.

"And his address?"

"That, I don't have."

"Don't you need it to send his check?"

"What check? We use Paypal. Anyway, his email is connor-dot-gray at gmail, if that helps."

Rebecca had dealt with trying to get a physical address from Google mail in the past. Not only was it difficult, but an amazing number of people lie to free e-mail providers about both addresses and phone numbers. "Can you tell me what Gray looks like?"

"Youngish, tall, thin, kind of geeky. To be honest, he's not anyone who'd ever be competition for the 'enticing bachelors'."

After Rebecca left the magazine, she called the number for Gray's cell phone. There was no answer.

～

Back at Homicide, Rebecca saw that not one of the three other men in the magazine had returned her call. She tried once more and again left messages.

She had asked for assistance from police in the Silicon Valley towns where Diego Bosque had three more stores to see if anyone had any idea about his whereabouts. So far, no one who knew him would file a missing person's report or do anything to declare him as a potential victim so that she could use all the power of the police department to find him. Everyone who knew him claimed Bosque kept to himself and they were not about to do anything that might upset him. Two days away from home, for Diego Bosque, who had condos in several states, was not a worry to them.

She reached for her phone to call the Santa Clara police to see if they had learned anything yet, but before she picked up the handset, she saw Richie's cousin, Angie, and Angie's mother, who Richie called "Zia Serefina," enter the bureau. Angie was a very attractive young woman with a stupendous wardrobe and killer shoes Rebecca envied. She was also so petite and feminine that when Rebecca stood beside her she felt as if she could try out as a female WWE wrestler—and would very likely get the job. Despite all that, Rebecca actually liked Angie, who was now married to Homicide Inspector Paavo Smith.

It was, in fact, Angie's connection to Paavo that caused Rebecca to meet Richie, which was the height of irony.

From the time Rebecca had first met Paavo when she was a

"trainee" homicide detective, she had developed a secret (or not so secret) crush on him. Later, when he met Angie, Rebecca kept thinking he'd come to his senses and date *her* instead, that she was much better suited to him. And now, Paavo and Angie were married, and she was seeing Richie.

But then, she reminded herself of the way Richie had walked out of the restaurant after they'd argued. She guessed their suitability or lack thereof was no longer an issue.

Paavo wasn't at his desk, but instead of Angie and Serefina seeing that and leaving, they walked straight over to her. Rebecca stood. "Angie, Serefina, how nice to see you. I think Paavo may be in court today."

"We know," Angie said. "We're actually here to see you. Do you have a minute?"

Uh oh. Rebecca had a good idea where this was going. "Please sit down." Rebecca pulled chairs together for them. "What can I do for you?"

"It's about Richie," Angie said.

Of course.

"We're worried about him," her mother chimed in. In looks, Serefina was a much rounder, older version of Angie—except that her shoes were chunky with low, stubby heels. "We need you to do something."

Rebecca's teeth clenched. "I see."

"Don't get Paavo in trouble," Angie said. "It really isn't his fault that he's terrible at hiding things from me. But I know Shig Tanaka was one of Richie's friends. In fact, I was the one who first brought him to Shig's restaurant after I discovered it. It was a marvelous place, and Shig was a fabulous chef."

Rebecca knew that Angie was also an excellent cook. That she'd never been able to find the right job to display her skill and knowledge of gourmet cooking was one of the banes of Angie's—and consequently Paavo's—existence.

Before Rebecca could reply, Serefina spoke up. "And he got his head cut off!"

"Shh! Mamma, it's not nice to say that in public!"

Rebecca's shoulders sagged. "So it's already out then, is it?"

"It's all over the news," Angie said, waving her arms as if to indicate it was truly everywhere.

"And we know," Serefina continued, "that someone set Richie's nightclub on fire!"

"Right after they tried to burn down Diego Bosque's store," Angie said.

"And we saw that horrible story in the magazine that talked about Richie along with those playboys! *Santa Maria, madre di Dio*," Serefina lifted her gaze to the ceiling, hands reaching upward.

"It was all lies, too." Angie assured Rebecca.

"He should sue them!" Serefina shouted, hands now in fists and eyes glowering.

"Richie doesn't deserve this!" Angie cried.

"So what are you doing about it?" Serefina demanded.

Two sets of dark brown eyes stared at her, waiting for an answer.

She swallowed. "We're trying to find any link—"

"Phone records?" Angie asked.

"Customers and suppliers?" Serefina asked.

"And their neighbors?" Angie suggested. "Do they go to the same clubs? Same bars? Interest in the same woman?" Angie gasped and looked at Serefina. "Maybe, Mamma, the whole thing is a love triangle gone wrong, and the article drove some woman right over the edge!"

"*Madonna mia!*" Serefina cried, eyes wide, as she crossed herself.

"Please!" Rebecca got to her feet. "Both of you. I appreciate your concern, but we're looking into all this. And lots more. I understand that you're worried about Richie and—"

"Well, aren't you?" Serefina asked as she and Angie also stood up. "From what I've heard, you two are close, no?"

"Mamma!" Angie cried. "That's not anything you should be talking about. At least, not here at Rebecca's work. Although"— she faced Rebecca—"we do hear that the two of you seem to be growing closer all the time. I'm so glad."

"We're just friends," Rebecca announced.

"Sure you are." Angie nudged her mother with her elbow. They smiled conspiratorially and gave each other a firm nod, then faced Rebecca again. "We completely understand."

After her last meeting with Richie, Rebecca had no business letting his relatives think there was anything more going on than there was. "There really is nothing between us. And if there ever was, it's over."

Angie's mouth dropped open. "Oh. I'm sorry to hear that."

"Although there are *some* who might be relieved," Serefina said, sotto voce, to Angie before turning to Rebecca again. "I'm sorry, too, but that's between you and Richie. We know it won't affect how you handle this case, and how you make sure he stays safe."

Their words, the way they looked at her, made Rebecca wish things had worked out differently with Richie. But all she said was, "I'll do my best. I assure you."

"*Bene.*" With that, they said their goodbyes and left.

Rebecca plopped herself back down in the seat. She wondered how many seconds would pass by before Serefina put in a call that would make Carmela Amalfi's day. Carmela, Richie's mother, had pretty much disliked Rebecca from the moment they first met. In Carmela's eyes, it was bad enough that she wasn't Italian or Catholic, worse that she was a cop, but then she became a complete persona non grata in Carmela's eyes after Richie was grazed in the arm by a gunshot while on a case with her.

The worst part of it was that Carmela had been right that he could have been killed. And Rebecca had played over and over in her mind what went wrong that had caused him to be in that kind of danger.

In a sense, she couldn't blame Carmela for hoping the two of them would break up. Now, the woman got her wish.

Rebecca decided to forget about all the Amalfis and went to the desk of Jamie Mills, a technical whizbang who worked in the Crime Scene Unit. She asked him to attempt to locate Diego Bosque via his phone, the GPS on his car, or his credit card use, but despite his "mad skillz" Jamie had no luck. It was as if Bosque, or someone, had gone to great lengths to see that he couldn't be found. Rebecca suspected Richie's friend, Shay, would have much better luck, but she was pretty sure that resource was as closed to her as Richie's friendship.

Sutter marched up to her as soon as she returned to her desk. "I'm on TV," he announced smugly.

"You are?"

"The beheading. Eastwood told me to talk to the reporters. I think I did pretty good, too."

Rebecca nodded. Eastwood liked using Sutter with the media because he could use more words to say absolutely nothing of any importance than anyone else in the department.

She told him she'd learned Tanaka and Bosque might have some business dealings with each other. When she heard Tanaka left the restaurant with Bosque the night before he died, she had reviewed security and traffic camera videos, but all it showed was both men driving away from Kyoto Dreams in their own vehicles, one a black Lexus, the other a black BMW. The cars soon disappeared from view, and while she picked them up a couple of times, both eventually disappeared from subsequent cameras.

She and Sutter had been doing extensive research on the backgrounds of the two men, looking for any kind of connection, any former trouble with the law, talking to people who knew them, searching for anything at all that could lead to someone wanting to brutally kill Tanaka and potentially to have kidnapped Bosque—or worse.

But so far, nothing had turned up.

She was again puzzling over Tanaka and Bosque's phone records when the autopsy, if you could call it that, on Tanaka's head hit her desk. She was stunned to find it showed a considerable amount of cocaine and alcohol in the bloodstream at the time of death. So much, in fact, that Tanaka was likely passed out or close to it when he was killed.

The report also showed that whatever caused death had only happened to the torso, very likely a gunshot or stabbing. Given Tanaka's state, it could have been inflicted by either a man or— and here she thought of Tanaka's odd love life—a woman.

Rebecca was pondering that when a call came in from Officer Lottie Hernandez in the city's Central Station.

8

———

If Rebecca were still a patrol officer, she'd want to work at Central Station. It had nothing to do with the physical space, which looked like Hollywood's version of an old, grubby precinct with a high front desk to meet the public, and a cluttered open room for the officers with mismatched, ancient desks. To make matters worse, it was at street level below a multi-storied parking garage. But as in real estate, it was all about the location. Central Station was on Vallejo Street between Grant and Stockton, an area where Chinatown blended with North Beach. Of the city's nine police stations, Central patrolled seven of the top ten San Francisco tourist attractions, including Fisherman's Wharf, Coit Tower, Union Square, Nob Hill, and Russian Hill, as well as the city's major hotels.

Rebecca once went up to the top level of the parking structure. The view of the city skyline with the bay, Alcatraz, the Golden Gate Bridge, and Coit Tower, was breath-taking.

She always had a spring in her step as she entered Central. As the desk clerk directed her to Lottie Hernandez's desk, she saw the officer smiling broadly while speaking to a man whose back was to Rebecca.

Hernandez spotted her and waved her forward. The man turned and stood. He looked like he had just stepped out of a Seagram's advertisement. He had seemed handsome enough in the magazine article, but it was nothing compared to the raw sexuality he exuded in real life. The thought crossed her mind that *this* was the kind of power and attraction that the tabloid had described.

"Mr. Brannigan, Inspector Mayfield," Rebecca said, shaking his hand as she reached the desk.

"Call me Moss." His blue eyes twinkled outrageously.

She smiled and then greeted Officer Hernandez and thanked her for calling. Hernandez showed the two of them to an interview room, and then she joined them. Looking at Brannigan—Moss—Rebecca didn't blame her. Talk about eye candy.

"I understand something happened that has worried you," Rebecca said. "Why don't you start at the beginning and tell me all about it."

"I know Lottie, I mean Officer Hernandez, has already heard all this ..." He flashed "Lottie" a megawatt smile. Rebecca couldn't help but stare. The man actually had deep dimples. She usually didn't care for dimples on a man, but on him they looked seriously sexy.

"No problem," Lottie said, beaming back at him. She was clearly not going anywhere. "You tell the Inspector all about it."

His piercing blue eyes met Rebecca's. "I probably wouldn't have thought too much about it if it weren't for the arson attacks and that terrible beheading. What a horror story! I can't even listen to the news anymore."

"Were you close to the men involved?" she asked.

"Not really. I met Pierre Fontaine through business connections. We put together a package deal for tourists. But I only met the others once."

"When was that?"

"Pierre asked me if I'd take part in a magazine article about bachelors who made it big in the city. Sounded like some great free publicity, so I said yes. Well, then, instead of what I was expecting, I learned *San Francisco Beat* was going to publish a hit piece on us. One of the guys involved, Richie Amalfi, got us together at Tanaka's restaurant to discuss it. We thought about suing—defamation, slander, libel, whatever. Lots of threats and terms were tossed around, but the more we talked, the more we realized the piece probably wouldn't hurt us for long. All of our businesses thrive on publicity. And you know what they say about publicity—it's all good. Well, not good if people get food poisoning at a restaurant, or drown on my tour boat, or get bed bugs in Fontaine's hotel. You know what I mean. But this—that a bunch of single guys are rich and interesting, and women (or in Travis's case, men) like to hang out around us—what's the problem? Finally, we decided to let the article get printed. If, as a result, our businesses suffered, then we'd revisit suing the tabloid. And we'd have proof that financial harm was done."

"In the course of the meeting," Rebecca asked, "did you get any sense of danger? That any of them were worried about their personal safety if the article was printed?"

"Not at all," Moss said. "That's why it came as such a shock to hear about the arsons and Shig's murder."

"Tell me, did the writer interview you?"

"He tried, but I wasn't about to talk to anyone from that rag."

"Did you ever see him?"

"No. He called. I never returned the calls."

"Okay." Rebecca drew in her breath. "Tell me what happened to you. Why are you afraid you're in danger?"

"I've got my tour boat but I also own a cabin cruiser. I use it for my own pleasure, up and down the coast mainly, although I have sailed all the way to Panama a couple of times. Fortunately, I've learned with my tour boat not to rely on any instruments but to always have back-up data. I headed out early this morning and planned to spend a couple of days cruising up around Mendocino when I saw a discrepancy in the fuel level. The shipboard instrument said the tank was full, which is where it was supposed to be. But my back-up gauge—the one that was supposed to be simply redundant, showed the tank down to only a quarter full. That made no sense, so I turned the cruiser around. It was all but empty by the time I docked. Once docked, I checked it over. I haven't found anything yet, but I know the fuel line and gas gauge were tampered with. That's the only explanation. I wanted to get to the police and report this before anything else happened. I also want to make sure if anything happens to me, it's not thought of as an accident. There's clearly some sort of maniac out there going after those of us in the magazine article. And I don't like it one bit!"

"I understand your worry," she said, her voice soothing. "I would suggest you double your private security efforts. I can ask that some patrol officers drive by your home as often as possible —and that'll help as long as you're home."

"What about police protection wherever I go?"

"Unfortunately, most police work is finding out who committed a crime, and not to prevent a personal attack."

"Bull shit! I see police protecting people all the time."

"At public events and for public officials, not one-on-one for private citizens. But I'll see what I can do. I'm only suggesting—"

"You're suggesting you sit around and twiddle your thumbs until I'm dead like Tanaka, or have my tour boat torched like Bosque and Amalfi's businesses were." He rose to his feet. "Thanks for telling me I just wasted my afternoon here, Officer."

"Wait." She stood and handed him her card. "You've been very helpful. I need you to tell me exactly what you find when you check your cruiser. I can send a crime scene team to the boat to look for any clues as to who might have done the tampering."

"Fat lot of good that'll do. Thanks for nothing."

He stormed from the station, leaving Lottie looking after him in bewilderment, and Rebecca steamed. Another egotistical "enticing bachelor" had just walked out on her.

And, adding insult to injury, Logan Travis and Pierre Fontaine still hadn't bothered to respond to her insistent calls.

9

———

Rebecca woke up to the insistent ringing of her doorbell. It was already nine o'clock, and the sun was streaming through the window. She sat up, unable to believe how she had slept so late, but working a murder case with only a head was quite labor intensive, especially when she'd stayed at it until after one in the morning.

The doorbell chimed again. She put on a bathrobe and slippers and went out to the breezeway to see who was bothering her. She pulled open the door and stared in shock. It was her Los Angeles-living, show business-aspiring, impossible-to-understand younger sister. "Courtney! What in the world are you doing here?"

Rebecca's younger sister was thirty years old, divorced, with no kids. She was beautiful—most of her good looks came naturally, but she had learned every trick in Hollywood's book to enhance what she was given. She didn't have an ounce of fat on her, and not much in the way of muscle either. Her bust line was as fake as her long, dark eyelashes, and the extensions in her dyed auburn hair.

She wasn't a mere Hollywood wannabe, but had acted in a

variety of parts over the past eight years. She hadn't yet, however, "hit it big." Her role that had the largest audience hadn't shown off her beauty at all. She'd been a zombie on TV's *The Walking Dead.*

"I was pretty sure you must be home when I saw that behemoth SUV of yours out in the alley." Courtney wheeled a carry-on bag into the breezeway toward Rebecca's apartment. "I tell you, the flight was okay, but the coffee was weak and all they gave us to eat was a tiny bag of pretzels. I'm starved and I'm getting a caffeine headache."

As they entered the apartment, Spike looked at Courtney and began non-stop barking and hopping from side to side.

"What in the world is *that?*" Courtney asked, pointing at the dog.

"That's Spike. Come on Spike, calm down. She's what's known as a sister."

But Spike wouldn't calm down until Rebecca picked him up. He had had a rough life before Rebecca found him at a crime scene where his owner had been killed, and he remained quite suspicious of strangers. "He doesn't know you, that's all."

"That's the ugliest dog I've ever seen in my life!"

"He is not!" Rebecca kissed his head.

"In what world? He's missing his freaking hair! And, what's with those awful pink spots? Are you sure it's even a dog?"

Courtney put her bag on the sofa and unzipped it.

"You're staying here?" Rebecca asked as she put Spike out in the yard—more for his sake than for Courtney's—and then filled the coffee maker with water. "This place is tiny for just me *and Spike.* What's going on?"

"I've stayed before with no problem." She took out a couple of blouses and a skirt on hangars. She shook them. "I'll hang them in the bathroom so steam from the shower will take out the wrinkles."

She no sooner stepped back into the kitchen area than Rebecca handed her a cup of coffee and proceeded to make a cup for herself.

"Already? Ah, you've got one of those fancy one-cup-at-a-time coffee thingies." Her eyes narrowed as she looked over the rest of the apartment. "Oh, my God! Look at that TV set. It's also new. And its plasma. And huge." Her head bobbed back and forth from the TV to the coffee maker. "Are you on the take?"

"Courtney! I can afford nice things now and then."

"After paying rent in San Francisco? Who do you think you're talking to?"

When Rebecca's coffee was ready, she sat at the small dinette table across from Courtney. "So, why don't you tell me what you're doing here."

Courtney put both hands on her coffee cup and waited a long moment before answering. "I'm hoping a story here will help me. A lot."

"A story? What do you mean?"

"I'm hoping to get a good news article on my own."

That made no sense to Rebecca. "Why are you doing news? You're an actress. Aren't you still with *Desperate World*?"

Courtney's eyes teared up. "No. My character killed herself last week. I've been trying to find something else, but everybody in Hollywood seems to want women who are in their early twenties, or even younger. It's disgusting. Thirty isn't old, but there aren't as many soaps as there used to be. I'm in the running for a couple of shows, but they need to wait a while. It's like, they don't want the public to say '*What's Delilah Morgan doing on this show?*' I mean, Delilah was quite popular, you know. A lot of people told me they watched *Desperate World* because of me. There was even some hate mail when I killed myself."

"I'm sure." Rebecca tried to sound sympathetic.

"Anyway," Courtney said as she blinked away her tears,

"there's going to be an opening coming up on *The Real Story*. It's a show that's dedicated to digging deep into news stories that have captured the public's imagination."

"I believe 'lurid' may be the term you're looking for," Rebecca said.

Courtney frowned. "You could say that. Anyway, the current lead has a drinking problem. They've kept it from the public, but she's going to be leaving 'to spend more time with her family' as they say." Courtney leaned forward and her forefinger pounded the table top. "I. Want. That. Job. And the best way I know to get it is to bring them the inside scoop on the murder case you're working on. Have you found the rest of the body yet?"

Rebecca just stared at her. "You do *not* mean that you want to dig into my case."

"I do," Courtney admitted. "I understand there were arsons, a death in one of those fires, a murder with no body, a missing bachelor, and they're all part of a juicy tabloid story. I want to call it '*The Bachelor* Meets *Survivor*.'"

"Great," Rebecca muttered.

"Little Miss Courtney Mays is just sure that this story will lead to her being named as a host on *The Real Story*. And you need to help her."

Rebecca hated it when her sister referred to herself in the third person almost as much as she hated the way Courtney had shortened their last name for "show biz" reasons. "I can't help you because I don't know who did it yet. I think you've wasted your time coming here. If you want, I'll let you know when I figure out who did it. Maybe then, you'll have a story."

"I'd like to meet the four bachelors you're able to find."

Rebecca blanched. "You aren't going to meet them through me!"

"Why not? You know me, I can usually get men to tell me all kinds of things. You know I can get hold of press credentials and use them to meet the surviving bachelors, but it'd be much easier if you'd simply introduce me as your sister, the Hollywood TV star. I'll take it from there. I mean, nobody tells the police anything, do they? I'm sure I'll find out stuff you could only dream of learning."

Rebecca didn't doubt that. "No."

"Damn it, Rebecca! You have all the luck. Can't you share a little of it with me?"

"I have luck? Are you kidding me?" Rebecca had never considered herself as being "lucky." Quite the opposite, in fact.

"This is a great story," Courtney insisted breathlessly. "It'll make your career, Rebecca. You might be Chief of Police some day. People care about it. If you catch the killer, you'll have saved all these great, handsome, eligible men. Too bad one was killed, and maybe two since we don't know why one of them is missing, but you can't have everything. And without their deaths, there'd be no case."

Rebecca looked at Courtney as if she were crazy, which she pretty much was. She was completely Hollywood in thought, word and deed—in other words, self-centered and willing to do whatever it took to get what she wanted.

Rebecca's phone buzzed. It was Sutter, telling her Pierre Fontaine was back in town. He had tried to talk to the guy, but Fontaine said he knew nothing and didn't want the police or anyone else bothering him. Sutter wanted to know if she wanted to give the arrogant French S.O.B. a try.

"I'll take it. He's at the hotel?" Rebecca asked as she looked at her sister. At the moment, interviewing Lucifer himself would be preferable to staying home arguing with Courtney.

She ended the call. "I've got to go out. You're wasting your time here. Enjoy the city. We can meet for dinner and catch up, but after that, I suggest you take the next plane home. When I solve this case, I'll be sure to let you know."

Courtney folded her arms and stared at her hard.

Rebecca was familiar with that look. It meant war.

La Colombe d'Or was a small, boutique hotel known only to people who could afford its outrageous rates. Its name was scarcely visible on a small brass plaque near the door. Despite all that, the elegant, flower-filled lobby, furnished to look like something from 1890s San Francisco, was buzzing with people.

Rebecca walked past the line of those waiting to check in. Approaching the harried desk clerk, she asked to speak to Pierre Fontaine. She slid her badge to the clerk rather than flashing it —she didn't want anyone to notice. The clerk nodded in gratitude at her discretion and rushed off.

In less than five minutes Pierre Fontaine emerged from the back room. His hazel eyes scanned the crowd and then fixed on her. One look and Rebecca could see why he was included in the magazine article. Like Moss Brannigan and, she had to admit, Richie, Fontaine's photos didn't do him justice. Nor was he hurt by the way he smiled at her—a mixture of both friendliness and something more: the look of a man appreciating the woman in front of him. To his credit, it didn't come across as a leer at all, but his gaze made Rebecca feel flattered, and despite herself, she stood a little straighter. If Fontaine could bottle that ability, he'd be a billionaire.

And considering the number of people in his lobby, he might be on the road already.

"I'm Pierre," he said as he approached. And of course he had a stomach curling sexy French accent to go along with the name, as well as dark brown wavy hair, captivating eyes, and an olive complexion. He wore a suit, but instead of stiff and businesslike, it looked soft, casual and shrieked "expensive."

"Inspector Rebecca Mayfield." She showed her badge.

He lifted his eyebrows as if impressed. "*Enchanté*, Inspector Mayfield. I received your calls, but your friend, Mr. Amalfi, told me how busy you are, and since I had nothing to add, I didn't want to waste your time. I thought I'd made it clear to your partner, as well. But, *ce n'est pas important.* You're here now. Let's go into my office."

"Fine." Rebecca spoke through clenched teeth at the thought of Richie's interference.

But then Fontaine's gaze shifted to somewhere over her right shoulder, and a bright, appreciative smile spread across his face. Rebecca turned to see what the attraction was. Her heart sank. She should have known.

"Look who's here!" Courtney said as she strolled towards them.

"Why are you here?" Rebecca asked.

"I'm looking for a room, of course," Courtney said before she turned her full attention on Fontaine with a dazzling smile.

His eyebrows were somewhere up near his hairline as he glanced at Rebecca. "So you know this lovely creature?"

"My sister, Courtney Mays." By way of warning, Rebecca quickly added, "She's with the press."

Courtney smiled brightly as she reached out her hand. "The LA press. I'm with a TV network."

Fontaine gave an appreciative murmur as the two shook hands. "We were just going into my office to discuss this *situation très terrible*. Won't you join us?"

Rebecca caught Courtney's gaze, letting her eyes narrow as she gave a small shake of the head.

Courtney faced Pierre. "I'd love to." She all but cooed the words.

Rebecca clenched her teeth so tight it caused a shooting pain in her jaw.

They no sooner entered Fontaine's office than a woman entered with a silver tray holding a coffee service and a platter of cream puffs and éclairs. Since Courtney had eaten only toast, and Rebecca nothing, the two couldn't turn down the pastries. Rebecca didn't know if it was because she was hungry or what, but she thought the éclair she was now eating was the most delicious she'd ever had. Courtney said so out loud.

"Thank you, ladies," Fontaine said. "My chef makes them fresh each morning for our guests. *Maintenant,* Inspector, what do you wish to know from me?"

Rebecca talked briefly about the murder, arsons, Bosque's disappearance, and Moss Brannigan's allegation of someone tampering with the fuel line on his cruiser. She admitted that she had not yet found any link between the incidents beyond the magazine article.

"That magazine article!" Fontaine exclaimed. "*Mon dieu!* I thought it would cause trouble, but I never dreamed anyone would die because of it."

His words were almost exactly the same as Richie's. Rebecca wondered exactly how much the two had talked about all this.

"What connection do you have to any of the men in the article?" she asked.

"I've known Richie and Shig for years, Moss Brannigan slightly, but I have no connection to the others. And fortunately, no one has bothered me or my hotel."

Courtney suddenly spoke up. "I'm really interested in how you became a hotel owner. I mean, running a hotel is usually kind of dull and staid. But from what I've read, you're none of those things."

He chuckled. "Actually, it's not so interesting. I come from a long line of hoteliers. My father put up the money for this one. He knew San Francisco would be a good investment."

"How fascinating," Courtney gushed.

Really? Rebecca thought.

But Pierre obviously liked Courtney's reaction. "Tell you what, since you are looking for a room, why don't you enjoy the comforts of La Colombe d'Or tonight as my guest?"

"Oh!" Courtney all but squealed. "I'd love—"

"She's staying at my place," Rebecca said. "She was only joking about the room. But it was very nice of you to offer. We should be going now. I may have more questions, but if you can think of anything that might help, please don't hesitate to call." She handed Fontaine her card.

"And here's mine," Courtney gave him a knowing smile. "As my sister said, please don't hesitate to call. Anytime."

"Of course," Pierre murmured.

Rebecca was mesmerized by the eye contact going on between the two. Fontaine looked at Courtney as if he was a cat and she was a canary. Little did he know that Courtney was much more of a hawk than a canary when prey was in sight. And he was definitely in her sights.

She hooked her arm in Courtney's and turned towards the door. "Thank you for your time, Mr. Fontaine. Goodbye."

"Call me Pierre, please. Until we'll meet again, ladies. *Au revoir.*"

10

———

Rebecca was fit to be tied. Last evening, she had hurried home from work to go to dinner with her sister and then see her off at the airport, only to find that Courtney had gotten a call from "Pierre" and had gone to dinner with him. And of course she never did get home last night.

Was her sister really that naïve? Did she truly not know that anyone of the bachelors in the article, except Shig Tanaka, was not only a potential victim but also a suspect? Courtney might end up, not with a story, but dead.

The more Rebecca thought about it, the more worried she became and finally phoned her sister around ten last night. Courtney told her to stop being "an old nag" and then hung up on her! Old? Is that what she was? And a nag?

Rebecca was tempted to call Richie to find out more about Pierre Fontaine's character, but had to admit that she was, very likely, overreacting. The two men were supposedly friends. And although Richie did seem to know some strange people, murderers didn't seem to be among them.

As she tried to fall asleep last night, she realized that while patricide was the word for murdering one's father, and matricide was murdering one's mother, she didn't know the term for murdering one's sister. She probably should learn it; she could imagine it turning up in her future.

And then, all day today, while her sister was being wined, dined, and probably much more by Mr. Frenchie Extraordinaire, Rebecca had spent her time canvassing neighborhoods in search of a date with a headless corpse.

She and Sutter had also questioned employees, suppliers, and friends of Shig Tanaka. The tedium was broken up only by turning on the news to see Sutter's interviews. The "head" came to be huge news, and the missing body ranked right up there with coverage of a missing Malaysian airliner some years back. It was sickening.

She even spent time with the Crime Scene Unit, hoping to prod them into finding some scrap of anything that might help. But, contrary to TV shows, it wasn't happening.

The only good news, if one could call it that, was she did learn the identity of the homeless victim, Benjamin Arthur Larkin—a man with a drug and alcohol problem who'd lived on the streets for the past twenty of his forty-five years.

Finally, she went home.

She opened the door to find Courtney sitting on the sofa, staring at her smart phone. Spike was crouched down on his stomach, on the floor, glaring at Courtney. When he saw Rebecca, he bared his teeth one more time at Courtney, and then trotted over to Rebecca to be petted. "What's up, Mister Spike?" Rebecca said, picking him up.

Courtney put down her phone. "That dog surely barks and growls a lot."

"I hadn't noticed." Rebecca said.

"I found out a lot about Pierre last night," Courtney said with a smile. "But not necessarily anything that will help your case."

Great, Rebecca thought. She could imagine Pierre Fontaine telling Richie all about it. She went outside with Spike.

She wished she hadn't thought about Richie. How was it Courtney had such an easy time around men she found attractive, while she got all discombobulated about them? Not around men in general—she worked with enough of them, but around men she "liked." But then she thought about several of the fellows she had dated and realized she had never been particularly ill at ease with any of them. It was just Richie. Not until she met Richie did she find herself irked and confused about her feelings in a way no man had caused her to be, ever.

What that meant, she had no idea. The one thing she did know was that it had nothing to do with undying love. You don't love someone you're tempted to shoot half the time.

She and Spike went back indoors so she could feed him his dinner.

"Are you going home today?" she asked Courtney as she dished out some Iams.

"Home? Why should I do that? I've made some great connections."

"Yes, Fontaine. So I've heard."

"Not to mention Moss Brannigan, Logan Travis, and the magazine editor, Liv Wong." Courtney wandered over to the kitchen area and watched Spike eat.

Rebecca froze, unable to process what she'd just heard. "Wait ... you expect me to believe that you met all those people today? Including Logan Travis? How did you do that?"

"Believe it or not, it's true. About Logan, I read a magazine article that said he liked to go to a deli in the Ingleside almost every day for a tuna salad sandwich on rye, so I went around the area until I found the right one and then offered twenty dollars to the deli clerk to shoot me a text the instant Travis showed up. I got the text, and I went. There he was, and we talked."

"But there are a lot of delis in the Ingleside."

"Not really. And even fewer that make a tuna salad sandwich on rye. It's called Raymond's New York Deli."

Rebecca sat down on one end of the sofa, Courtney on the other. "So, what did Travis say?"

"Well, he is definitely good looking, but he's also kind of nuts."

"But about the murders ..."

"He's worried about them, but other than that, he claimed to know nothing. It was really quite disappointing, especially after I wasted twenty bucks. But I did get a selfie with him so that might be worth something."

"How did you get him to talk to you?" Rebecca asked.

"I ordered a tuna salad on rye myself and started by saying I was surprised anyone else ate them."

Rebecca shook her head. Courtney was beyond unbelievable. "And Moss Brannigan? You saw him?"

"Yeah. Down at his tour boat company. The man glommed onto me when I told him I'm connected to TV in LA. Oh, my God, what a publicity hound! He's the opposite of Logan Travis. I couldn't get him to shut up. But I did get a lot of good photos of him and his boat. It seems his business has picked up quite a bit lately. They say all publicity is good in one way or another. I guess he's living proof."

"So I've heard," Rebecca murmured.

"Pierre's finding the same thing. His hotel is handling more reservations than ever." Courtney shook her head. "Poor Pierre. All this has him rather spooked. He's got bodyguards, you know."

"That's good. If this case doesn't get resolved soon, I may have to do a proper interview with him."

Courtney smiled. "I don't blame you for wanting to get to know him better. He'd be a real prize."

"I'm sure. But as far as I'm concerned, he's all yours."

"Maybe. Keep in mind there's another bachelor I haven't met," Courtney said. "Pierre told me Richie Amalfi's nightclub is re-opening tonight. I can't wait to meet him! Why don't you come with me, Rebecca?"

"I really don't think—"

"Please! You must! Pierre hinted that he might show up tonight as well, and it might be awkward for me trying to juggle the two of them."

Rebecca's mouth dropped open.

"After all, I wouldn't mind spending time with Pierre again if things with Richie don't work out. Say you'll come with me."

Rebecca stared at her a moment, shut her mouth, and said, "Fine. I'll come with you."

11

———————

It had been years since Rebecca and Courtney went anywhere together. Not since they were in Idaho as a matter of fact. Rebecca left Boise after breaking up with her fiancé—the fellow from the neighboring farm. At the time, she'd been devastated. Now, if she ever saw him, she'd tell him how thankful she was that things hadn't worked out between them and she'd been able to experience life as a cop and a homicide detective. She was seeing more of life and death than she had ever thought possible, and despite how hard and brutal and, yes, often lonely her life felt at times, she never regretted a minute of it.

Once Rebecca agreed to go to Big Caesar's, Courtney insisted they make a quick run to Nordstrom's. There, Courtney bought a new, low-cut silver dress that complemented her long auburn hair, and talked Rebecca into splurging on a slinky black number.

"We're looking pretty good, sister," Courtney said, now standing in front of the mirror in Rebecca's bedroom. She spritzed some of the perfume in the air above Rebecca's head.

"Oh, that smells good!" Rebecca said. "What is it?"

"Don't you recognize it? L'Air du Temps. You used to wear it when you lived at home, and I'd steal some when you weren't looking. I spotted it when I was downtown today and bought it just for you."

"I do remember." She held out her wrist and got a little more. "I wonder if old Eddie was more in love with this perfume than me. He certainly found someone else to marry soon after I left the state."

"He was such a jerk," Courtney said. "I'm really glad you didn't marry him."

"Now you tell me!"

The two continued to laugh over old times as Rebecca drove them to Big Caesar's.

But as soon as she stepped into the nightclub and contemplated facing Richie after the way they'd parted, she actually felt nervous. The band was playing "I Got It Bad and That Ain't Good." She felt as if she should make it her theme song.

The club was packed with people. Clearly, the publicity had also helped Richie. "Come this way," she said to Courtney as she headed towards the bar area.

"Oh, I like this music! What a neat place. I can't wait to meet Richie!" Courtney all but danced her way across the room as they squeezed through the crowded dance floor.

The bar area had become a bit of an upscale pickup spot for the over thirty set, and Courtney's appearance didn't go unnoticed. Rebecca knew she was usually eyed as she headed towards the bar, but it was nothing compared to the way she felt now as she walked beside her saucy, red-haired sister who, as an actress, certainly had learned how to draw plenty of attention to herself.

They ordered drinks and four men instantly surrounded them, all asking to pay. Courtney was eating up the attention and greeting each fellow while Rebecca kept watch for the one she wanted to see. He usually showed up almost immediately. She planned to apologize. Nothing more; but she owed him that.

Courtney was willing to let someone buy their drinks, but Rebecca refused and put her money on the bar. The bartender took it ... and still no Richie.

After making some inane conversation with a lawyer, and refusing his suggestion that they dance, Rebecca asked the bartender if Richie was in the club that evening. He was.

Richie could scarcely believe that Rebecca had actually come into his club tonight. At first, he was elated to see her—maybe she'd come to bury the hatchet, to wish him well after his post-arson renovation. But then he saw what he assumed was the real reason she'd ventured into his lair.

The family resemblance was there, but nothing more. Her somewhat famous sister, Courtney Mays, was what Rebecca would be if she "went Hollywood." Courtney was beautiful, he had to admit, but carefully put together—stylized to near-perfection—while Rebecca's beauty was more natural and far more subtle. He wondered what it meant that he normally was drawn to women with Courtney's dazzle, but now it meant little to him.

He was tempted to go back into his office, but his "grand reopening" meant he had to meet-and-greet. Fortunately, Big Caesar's was a big club. He carefully made his way to the opposite end of the club, far from the bar, and stayed near the door where—as one of the city's infamous enticing bachelors—he could welcome his customers in style.

It didn't take long for Pierre Fontaine to show up. He got a table for them. He and Courtney were acting like turtledoves, to Rebecca's disgust, while she sat there feeling like a fifth wheel.

"I guess Richie Amalfi is busy," Rebecca said. "I don't think you'll be meeting him tonight, Courtney."

"You didn't meet him yet?" Pierre said, surprised. "Why not? He was at the door when I arrived and directed me towards you."

Rebecca was speechless.

"He knows me?" Courtney said. "How exciting! I can't wait to meet him. Find him for us, Pierre, please."

"Maybe I should be jealous?" he said with a wink.

Rebecca couldn't take it. She picked up her handbag and then rose to her feet. "I'm leaving. You're clearly in good hands, Courtney. I'll see you later."

"Ah!" Pierre said looking past her. "He's coming now."

Rebecca turned around and saw Richie heading towards them. Her breath caught. His gaze was on her, but his brows were crossed, his mouth firm.

"Be still my heart," Courtney murmured.

Richie's eyes didn't leave Rebecca's until he reached their table. Then he nodded at Pierre and faced Courtney.

"Richie Amalfi!" she said. "I've so wanted to meet you."

"My sister," Rebecca told him. "Courtney Mays."

He shook Courtney's hand. "The famous Courtney Mays," he said, with a warm smile. "I've heard much about you. It's nice to finally meet." He turned to Pierre. "How are you so lucky, my friend, as to be with two such beautiful women?" he said as they, too, shook hands.

"Please join us," Courtney said.

He grabbed an empty chair and put it close to Rebecca. "You look beautiful tonight," he said as he sat.

"Thank you," she said softly. "And Big Caesar's looks great, too."

"That's good of you to say," he told her.

Rebecca could see Courtney taking in every word, looking curiously at the two of them. She felt awkward under her sister's scrutiny.

A waitress brought Richie a drink that looked like a gin and tonic with lime. Rebecca knew it had no gin, since he almost never drank when working.

Richie put his hand on the back of Rebecca's chair as he faced Courtney. "Pierre tells me you're looking into the arsons and murder."

"He did?" She glanced at Pierre with surprise. Clearly, Rebecca thought, her sister knew nothing about Richie's network of sources. "Pierre's right. I'm here to do a TV news story with Rebecca's help, but"—she widened her eyes innocently—"so far, she doesn't seem to want me involved. I've had to take things into my own hands as much as possible."

"And I suspect Rebecca doesn't like you doing that," he said.

"No." Courtney grimaced. "She can be pretty bossy."

He glanced at Rebecca and she could see how very much he wanted to grin. He kept looking at her even as he spoke to Courtney. "Maybe she's just worried about you and wants to keep you safe."

Again, Courtney studied the two of them. Rebecca couldn't help but suspect that not even self-centered Courtney could miss that something was going on between them. "You two know each other pretty well, don't you?" Courtney asked.

"Richie and I are just friends," Rebecca said quickly.

Pierre leaned close to Courtney and in a stage whisper said, "They know each other well. Believe me."

Richie scowled at him, then glanced again at Rebecca. "I like to think we're good friends."

That was the last thing she expected him to say after the way they'd parted. But he couldn't possibly mean anything by it. "We've worked a number of cases together," she further explained.

Richie looked into her eyes. "We did well. A good team."

Pierre chuckled. "See what I mean?" he asked Courtney.

Courtney nearly choked on her whiskey sour. "I had no idea! Are you two like that TV show with the lady cop and the writer who goes around working cases with her?"

Rebecca was horrified. "No. Not at all."

"I kind of like that," Richie said with a grin. "Maybe I should start coming along on all your cases."

"It's bad enough having you around when there's a reason for you to be there!" Rebecca said.

"Oh, I've always got a reason to be there." He then called over a cocktail waitress. "Bring us a platter of appetizers, please."

In little time, a generous platter of hot appetizers appeared. Rebecca figured someone else's order was diverted to the night-club owner's table.

As they ate, Courtney questioned him, although her questions quickly went from asking about the murders, about which he gave very little information, to asking how he and Rebecca met. She was particularly interested in the case where they got to know each other fairly well—the one where Richie was accused of murder and had the chutzpah to ask Rebecca, the homicide detective handling the case, to help him.

"Are you crazy?" Courtney asked. "I know my sister. I don't understand how she didn't arrest you on sight."

"She did. And the things she can do with handcuffs!"

Rebecca glared. "No! It was you who ..." She stopped when she saw him trying hard not to laugh. She faced Courtney. "He's right. I did arrest him."

"But my air of innocence," he added, "saved the day."

Courtney was finding Rebecca's discomfort hilarious when "It Had to be You" started to play. Richie faced her. "I know this is one of your favorite songs. What do you say? For friendship?"

She hesitated. "Oh, I don't think—"

"Yeah," he said, taking her hand and pulling her to her feet. "You do."

She glanced over at Courtney and realized she didn't want to make a scene. Before she knew it, she was in his arms. She liked being there again; liked it a lot. "Before you say anything else," she told him, "I'm sorry for the way I talked to you at the steak house. It was uncalled for."

"Maybe you were right."

"No. I know you better than that."

"About the connection with the article."

She didn't say a word because his arms tightened and all she could think about was his nearness. She'd never known anyone who both intrigued and confused her so completely. She shut her eyes as she held him, letting the music and the words fill her.

When the song ended, they dropped their arms and simply faced each other a long moment before returning to the table.

"Your phone was making strange noises," Courtney said.

Rebecca took it out of her purse. The missed call was from Homicide Inspector Luis Calderon. He never called unless it was really important. "I'd better take this."

She stepped out of the ballroom to the hall and phoned him back. "Luis, what's up?"

She felt as if ice water had been poured down her back as she listened to his words.

Back at the table, her face must have shown her distress because Richie offered her his hand as she sat. She took it, one hand tightening on his, and her other hand reached for Pierre's.

"They found Diego Bosque." She swallowed hard looking at

the two men with her and wondering how much danger they were in. "He was garroted in his car."

"Garroted? *Qu'est-ce que c'est ça?*" Pierre asked.

"A wire, around his neck," Rebecca said. "I'm so sorry."

Richie and Pierre looked at each other, disbelief and worry in their eyes. "Damn," Richie said. "Call your security before you leave here."

Pierre nodded.

"You, too," Rebecca told Richie. "This is nothing to take chances with." She squeezed both their hands. "Stay safe. I've got to go to the crime scene. I'll drop Courtney off at home. I'd better do a quick change of clothes. It's going to be a long night."

Courtney glanced at Pierre who seemed lost in thought, then nodded at Rebecca.

"We'll walk you out to your car," Richie said as they all stood.

"No. We're fine. You two need to do what's necessary to take care of yourselves. I'll talk to you when I learn more."

Richie sat back down, as did Pierre. Rebecca realized it was one of the few times he'd ever done what she asked. Strangely, she didn't feel good about it.

Rebecca drove to the parking garage underneath Union Square in the heart of San Francisco's downtown. A uniformed officer spotted her waving her badge and directed her down two floors. She easily found the crime scene, not because of the officers standing around a black Lexus, but because of the photo-snapping crowd of gawkers.

The Crime Scene Unit was at work. The medical examiner had come and gone, and Luis Calderon and his partner, Bo Benson, were just finishing up. They would complete their canvass of the area and then share their information with

Rebecca and Sutter. This case had just gotten big enough that Lt. Eastwood ordered all four detectives to stay on it.

Rebecca peered inside the Lexus. The victim looked to be in his mid-to-late thirties, light brown hair, slim and trim. His face was florid, his eyes open and streaked with broken blood vessels. His clothes had been soaked with blood, now dried. Around his neck was a wire that cut into his flesh, cutting through his neck and severing his carotid arteries. The blood and scratches on his neck along with the blood on his fingers and nails were most likely from trying to grab the garrote and pull it from his neck.

Rebecca took a step back. Although the victim's face was red and disfigured from his death struggles, there was no doubt in her mind that she would have recognized him. She had looked at his photograph too many times this past week.

She picked up the garage's ticket stub.

Assuming Diego Bosque had tried to leave within a few hours of entering the garage, he had been in this car, dead, for two days.

12

———————

A little after one a.m., Rebecca made it back to her apartment.

Courtney was curled up asleep on the sofa, the TV on, but woke up as soon as she heard the front door shut. She sat up. "I was getting worried about you."

"I'm fine," Rebecca said wearily. "Glad to be home."

The two decided Courtney should share the queen-size bed with Rebecca. She'd find it more comfortable than the sofa, and they had shared a bed many times when growing up. As they put clean sheets on it, and got into their nightclothes, Rebecca told Courtney a little about the crime scene.

"It's such a shame," Courtney said. "When you told Pierre and Richie that another friend had been murdered, it made it all much more real to me. Before then, I'll confess, it was like a movie—all fake."

"I wish it were fake," Rebecca said. "No such luck."

The two soon fell into bed, exhausted, but once the lights were off, Courtney rolled onto her side facing Rebecca. "Okay, tell me about Richie."

"What do you mean?"

"What's he like? What do you know about him? And how do you feel about him?"

Rebecca didn't want to touch the last question, so she told Courtney a little about Richie's past, about him growing up in North Beach, how his father had been killed when he was young, how he was a self-made man, and that when he finally wanted to settle down, his fiancée died in an auto accident. It took a few years and two very good friends to pull him out of a depression after that.

"Not an easy life," Courtney said. "The way you talk about him, I think you really care about the guy."

"I do care about him, but that's as far as it'll ever go. He's told me as much, especially with me being a cop. It scares him, and I understand that completely. Also, he's not my type."

"Oh. Not at all. Anyone can see that." If Courtney had spoken any more tongue-in-cheek, she'd have a hole in the side of her face. Courtney shifted to lie on her back. "You know what your problem is?"

"I know you're going to tell me."

"It's that you've walled your emotions up so thoroughly, you don't know what you feel. You gave your heart to two guys that people told you were good, true men, and they weren't. Or, at least, they weren't right for you. And now you're seeing someone that 'people' say is wrong for you, someone you shouldn't trust at all—at least that's what *SF Beat* would have you believe. Let me tell you, you can't listen to others."

"But—"

"No buts. I think you actually do trust him, which has only confused you all the more because you believe you can't trust your own instincts. After all, you've been wrong twice already, right?"

"I'm not—"

"And even worse, you're a control freak. And you're bossy. I swear, when I heard you'd become a cop, I howled. I told everyone that was the perfect job for you."

"I am not bossy!"

"Oh, yes. And even your boyfriends, as much as you felt they left you, I think you may have given a bit of a shove."

"I never—"

"And now you've met someone you can't control."

"I don't want to control him."

"That, I do believe. You enjoy the challenge of the guy."

"This is all such nonsense, Courtney."

Courtney laughed aloud. "Sure it is. Look, I've been married, divorced, and I've considered getting remarried more times than I can count. I've made some lulus of mistakes with men in my life, but that hasn't stopped me from looking. I suspect I'm more determined than ever to find the right guy. You think Richie's not your type? Who was your type? Farmer Eddie or that jerk you were seeing when you first came to the city who ran off like a scared rabbit when you got shot. Believe me, if you were hurt, Richie would be there for you. I can see it in him."

"He would be, for something like that. But as far as a long-lasting, committed relationship, he's not looking for that—at least, not from me. He's told me as much."

"I'm sure he has. The problem is, you've listened to his words. And I suspect he's listened to yours. Rebecca, you say really hurtful things when you're scared."

"Scared? Me?"

"Yes, you!" Courtney said. The way her words were slowing down, Rebecca could tell that she was almost asleep, but still, she murmured. "From what I'm seeing in this, with each other, you're both cowards."

13

At Homicide the next morning, Sutter let Rebecca know Moss Brannigan had called and said he'd found a hole in his gas line. He was sure someone had put the hole in it, and was trying to kill him. Since Rebecca hadn't gotten along with him, Sutter decided to step in. The marina where the boat was docked had all kinds of security. If someone had tampered with Brannigan's cruiser, he would have worked hard to avoid cameras. Sutter planned to review the security footage when he had time.

Now that Diego Bosque was found dead, the news media was going crazier than ever covering the story of the "bachelor murders." Lt. Eastwood, rather than Sutter, was holding press conferences.

Whoever killed Bosque had disarmed the GPS system in his car and removed the SIM card from his phone. Rebecca had access to Bosque's phone records and could get his text messages, but she was stymied as far as any encrypted messages the phone might contain. Not even the super techs in the Crime Scene Unit could crack the phone.

Also, just as she'd warned Richie and Pierre after learning of

Bosque's death, she also had to warn the two other enticing bachelors. She had Sutter contact Moss Brannigan while she again tried to reach Logan Travis, but his phone sent her, as usual, to voice mail. She tried to find a secretary, an office, or any other way to reach him, but had no luck.

She and Sutter went again to Bosque's apartment. This time, they were able to enter it and search for any clue as to a motive for his murder, or a lead on any suspects. The strangest finding was many boxes of black vests. They weren't your grandfather's vest, but attractive ones that she imagined looked good on slim, younger men. But why so many boxes?

The vests were all made in China, according to the packaging.

The more Rebecca learned about the victims in the case, the more confusing everything became. She couldn't remember dealing with anything like this before. Arsons, murders, and a whole variety of different businesses. Nothing made sense.

She was also so sick and tired of being ignored, berated, and walked out on by these enticing (*hah!*) bachelors, that, while Sutter headed back to Homicide, she decided to drive to Logan Travis's home. She planned to insist he talk to her, or she'd bring him in for obstruction of justice. It was already evening, so he should be home.

The exterior of his home was surprisingly humble-looking. Something told her the millionaire's interior wouldn't be nearly so modest. She rang the doorbell and knocked loudly several times, but there was no answer. No lights were on that she could tell.

She stood outside the house pondering what to do next.

The Ingleside district wasn't very far away from Twin Peaks, where Richie's home was located, and since he knew Travis, he could most likely reach the man. But she was conflicted. That was what happened when a person allowed her private life to get mixed up with her professional one.

She stewed over what to do a little longer, then got into her car and headed for Richie's house.

He lived on a narrow street near the top of Twin Peaks, one of the city's more expensive areas. As she reached his home, she saw that the lights were on inside. Normally, she would have pulled into his driveway, but that was something friends did, and this was a business-oriented visit. She saw a parking space a couple of houses down on the opposite side of the street and took it.

The street level of his house held the garage and a storage area while the house proper was on the second level. She walked up the long flight of stairs to the front door and rang the bell.

When he didn't open the door, she phoned his land line. She could hear his phone ringing.

"Yes?" he said.

It wasn't exactly the friendliest greeting she'd ever heard. "Open your door, Amalfi."

He did. He looked surprised to see her. She walked into his living room. It was a large room, dominated by a picture window that gave a view of the east side of San Francisco, from the downtown to the waterfront, the Bay Bridge, and then beyond to the East Bay hills. Another wall held a gas-operated fireplace, which was now lit to ward off the chill of the foggy night air.

"I'm here because of my cases," she said quickly.

"I see." His gaze was shuttered, impossible to read. "Okay, so what do you want to know?"

"Can we sit?" she asked as she moved towards the sofa.

He nodded and sat in the chair facing it. She took the sofa. He didn't offer her any wine, beer, or coffee, which wasn't like him. But then, she had said this was business. She quickly told him about her earlier meeting with Moss Brannigan, and his discovery today that someone had, indeed, tampered with his fuel line. "That means attacks were made on four of the six of you, with two deaths."

"That damned magazine." Richie angrily folded his arms. "We didn't expect it to turn out the way it did, of course! No one expected that. What the hell."

"I never learned how the article came about," she said.

A moment passed before he answered. "I was at Tanaka's restaurant having lunch with Pierre. The restaurant was surprisingly empty, so Tanaka joined us and we got to talking about how this economy is the pits. I said the cost of advertising was my biggest problem. It's ridiculously high in this city. Pierre said we needed free PR, and that we should go on some reality TV show. I suggested, *The Bachelor,* and the idea grew from there. We thought a magazine article would be great PR, but we figured three guys wasn't enough. Pierre said he knew the owner of the Golden Gate Tour Boat company, Moss Brannigan, who Pierre claimed looked like someone who'd stepped out of the pages of a romance novel about sea captains and pirates. Tanaka said he knew the owner of Easy Street, where a lot of the new tech millionaires shop. And I knew Logan Travis who's part of that Silicon Valley crowd, plus he's gay. We thought we had a good mix. I pitched the idea to a few reporters I know, suggesting a puff piece about six single guys working to make it big in the city, and succeeding. I even gave them the names. They sounded like they thought it was a great idea."

"That was no puff piece."

"I know. I have no idea how it ended up at *San Francisco Beat.* All I know is someone took our good idea and turned it into a bucket of spit. And now, two of the guys are dead." He ran his fingers through his hair, his gaze downcast.

"The question is," she said, "how did the idea get changed?

Do you know the writer or the editor? Did you contact anyone connected with the *Beat*?"

"You think I'm nuts or what?"

"Sorry." She thought about his story. "The editor of the *Beat* told me she once worked for *Sunset Magazine*. Do you have any connections there?" The large, high-circulation magazine was based near Silicon Valley.

Richie frowned. "I do. I pitched the story to a *Sunset* writer. Why not go big-time, right? She's idiot enough to have given it to the *Beat*."

"I suspect that's what happened," Rebecca said. "But I also heard you knew about the change in tone for the story before it was printed."

Richie told her how his bouncer, Lenny, found the writer, Connor Gray, in his club bothering a couple of the cocktail waitresses. "As Lenny was ready to boot the guy out, he told him he had a first amendment right to be there because he was working on an article about me for the *Beat*. God, what a filthy rag. Anyway, I know a guy who's dating the copy editor there, and she sent me the draft of the story. That's when I called a meeting to let the other guys know what had happened."

"Did any of the men give you an indication the article could pose a danger for them?"

"No."

"No engagements that might be broken, or business deals that might go south?"

"No one said a word."

"When I spoke to a detective in Kyoto after Tanaka's death," she said, "he mentioned that Tanaka had been investigated for ties to the Yakuza, but was cleared."

Richie scowled. "Cleared? Did he also tell you the Yakuza's tentacles often reach to Japanese officials? Especially low-level local ones? A clearance might not mean a whole lot." He continued. "God, if the Yakuza is involved ... Such a group would explain the violent deaths, but not the arsons."

"True, unless they want to get involved in your work as well, and the arson was a warning."

His chin lifted a bit as he said, "I doubt it."

She wanted to ask why, but decided she might not like his answer. His connections, she suspected, ran deep and wide. Instead, she asked, "Did Tanaka ever give the slightest hint some sort of criminal activity was going on?"

He thought a moment. "Not in so many words. I'd heard rumors about him and some shady business associates, but not anything specific. In any case, I tried to ignore them—not my business—and yet I always had a feeling something big was going on that he didn't like, something probably illegal. He'd make jokes about going away, hiding even, somewhere that no one knew his name. I tried to let him know I might be able to help, but he never asked. And I never pressed the point. Like I said, it was none of my business."

"Thank God he didn't go to you if the Yakuza is involved," she said.

"Maybe. Or, maybe he'd still be alive."

She changed the focus. "What about the other two men?" she asked.

"Pierre introduced me to Brannigan, and I've known Travis about a month."

"How did you meet Travis?" she asked.

"He asked me to help him with something."

"With what?"

"Security. It started small, but every week he called back to get a bigger and better system. The whole Silicon Valley crowd is a nest of vipers and intrigue with people poaching each other's ideas and patents all the time."

She nodded. "He wouldn't answer any of my phone calls or

messages. When you speak to him, would you ask him to call me?"

"Sure."

She had run out of things to ask him about. She stood. "You've given me a lot. Thank you. I should get back to work."

"So, the grilling is finally over." It was as if a door had been slammed shut. His face lost all warmth. "Okay."

"Be careful," she said.

He remained motionless ... and emotionless.

She left the house. As she walked down his front steps, she realized how much she missed being with him. Not the Richie she'd just interrogated, but the warm guy she'd come to know. She missed the excitement being around him had always brought her. But now that the tabloid article had caused this rift, she had no idea how to end it. She put the key into the ignition of her Ford Explorer, but then pulled it back out. What if she went back to his house and asked if they could start over? Would that help, or ultimately, only lead to bigger and worse complications?

She reached towards the ignition again, then stopped. Maybe she should check her messages, and if nothing was urgent, she'd go back to see him. She knew she wanted to. And this time, she wouldn't immediately announce she was there *only* because of her murder investigations.

She was waiting for her new messages to load when she saw a car turn onto the street. It drove by Richie's house, then turned around at the end of the block and drove down the street again. She slumped down in the car seat watching it. The car parked just past Richie's. She told herself the driver must be someone looking for one of his neighbors. A visitor. That's all.

The driver got out of the car and stood there a moment, then crossed to Richie's side of the street. He disappeared momentarily, but then the glow from a street lamp cast a faint outline of someone near Richie's house. It was the driver, she was sure. He was tall, dressed in dark clothes, and a hoodie. She didn't like what she was seeing.

He walked along the side of Richie's house, the side next to the garage, and then disappeared. A fence and gate were there, leading to Richie's back yard. She got out of her car and followed, gun in hand.

The gate was still shut, but she didn't see the man anywhere. She phoned Richie.

"What?"

Wow, but he sounds angry ... or hurt. "Someone is lurking around your house. He may have snuck into your yard."

"You're just full of good news."

"Shut the lights and let me in."

He hung up.

The door was slightly ajar when she reached it. She entered the darkened house.

"You sure someone is out there?" He sounded dubious as he quietly shut and locked the door.

She stepped close enough to make out his features in the moonlight shining through the window. "All I can tell you," she whispered, "is that I saw a man approach your side gate and then disappear. He may have climbed over it. I didn't want to take any chances."

"Chance of what?"

"That you might be hurt!" With that admission, she saw a relaxing of the hard line of his mouth, a softening around his eyes.

She walked into the kitchen and stopped. The back door was mostly glass with eight window panes, and on both sides of it were large windows. It gave the kitchen a lot of sunlight during the day making it a warm, inviting spot to cook and eat. Now, it offered a good view of the deck, and the moonlit yard.

Richie stepped up behind her, his hand on her shoulder. As they waited with nothing happening, he leaned close. "How long do we wait?"

"We need to be sure," she whispered.

"Yes, we do," he said. She wondered for a moment if he was referring to more than the prowler, but then he added, "What do we do if he's out there?"

"I have a gun, remember," she whispered.

His hand tightened slightly on her shoulder. "You aren't the only one."

She was pondering the various ways she could take that statement when she heard a sound outside. She froze. "Did you hear that?"

He let her go and took a few steps closer to the window for a better view of what was happening in the garden. He moved one hand to the back of his waist—a common place for a holster for a small handgun. Of course, she realized, he would have a gun in the house, and probably more than one, even if he couldn't get a concealed carry license in this city.

Suddenly, a face shadowed within a hoodie appeared outside the kitchen window. She jumped, startled, and it seemed Richie did the same.

The figure stared inside the house no more than a split second and then turned and ran.

Rebecca pushed past Richie, flung the kitchen door open and stuck her head out, ready to hurl herself back indoors if she saw a gun pointed at her. Instead, she saw the hooded man running down the steps to the yard. "Stop, police!"

"Rebecca, no!" Richie reached for her, but she was already running down the stairs from the deck to his lawn and garden.

The intruder ran across the yard to the high fence.

"Stop or I'll shoot!" Rebecca shouted.

He boosted himself over the fence as Rebecca hit the bottom

step. Richie was right behind her. She reached the fence and was about to scramble up and over it when Richie grabbed her.

"*What are you doing?*" she yelled. "Let go of me!"

"No. It's too dangerous."

"I know what I'm doing." She was furious.

"I don't give a damn." He pulled her away from the fence, gripping her wrists.

"It's my *job*. I could have caught him."

"You have no back-up." They were nose to nose. "So no, you don't go running after a killer alone. For all you know, this could be a contract job. Which would make him a pro, which would mean he'd as soon put a bullet in you as not."

She would have continued to fight him except that she became too aware of his nearness, of how tightly he was holding her. Ironically, she had once thought that getting closer to him, even having sex with him, would make it easier to forget about him—that the mystery and excitement would be gone. Instead, she found it more difficult than ever. His touch, now, reminded her of all she was missing. And the change in his expression, in his eyes, told her he had the same awareness.

Her breathing quickened as she fought against her instincts. "Let go."

He did, and stepped back, running a hand over the back of his head as if needing to do something, anything, rather than let himself reach for her again.

They went back into the kitchen, and Richie handed her a beer as he called Shay, telling him to get over there to help him figure out what was going on.

When he hung up, he got a beer for himself. Rebecca could still feel the adrenaline pumping through her. "I might have ended this, right here and now," she said.

"You don't know that."

"Could you recognize him at all?" she asked. "Height? Stance? Anything?"

"You saw him, too. I couldn't make out anything, except that he's tall and athletic enough to get over a six-foot high wooden fence."

"He was wearing gloves." She rubbed her forehead, trying to think of something helpful. "Even if I called someone at work, there's probably no way they could figure out who he was. And with that hoodie pulled low, I suspect your security cameras couldn't pick up his face, anyway."

He circled her, pacing and nervous. "Yeah, well, all that's well and good because one cop trudging through my house is bad enough."

"Real nice, Richie." Her temper, her frustration at him, at the whole situation, flared. "What if I hadn't seen him? If I hadn't called you? He might have snuck in here, or shot you through a window. I mean, anything could have happened!"

He faced her, standing close. "Why did you? I would have thought you'd be long gone."

She didn't answer.

He continued to wait.

She changed the subject. "You can't stay here. It's not safe."

"Yeah, I can. It's my house."

"It's too dangerous and you can afford to go elsewhere."

"You'll come with me?"

She was stunned by his question. "Of course not!"

Something in his gaze shifted, and she felt the tension in the room go up several notches as, without losing her gaze, he put down the beer and walked towards her. She could feel her pulse quicken and she knew, despite what she had said, she just might go anywhere with him.

Before he reached her, however, his phone buzzed. It was Shay, calling to say he'd be there in ten to fifteen minutes, and that he'd called a bodyguard friend of his who would arrive about the same time.

Richie ended the call and faced her. "For now, Rebecca Rulebook, we'll do things your way. Fill Shay in on all the details. The analysts at the SFPD are okay, but none have an MBA from the Wharton School of Business the way he does, or are such whizzes at figuring out financial schemes. And the more I think about what's going on here, the more I think the businesses are the key."

Rebecca agreed.

"And then you can go about your routine of searching for clues and following the evidence." His eyes turned serious. "But one of these days, you're going to have to make up your mind, once and for all."

She understood that he wasn't only talking about her murder investigations.

14

───────

On her desk the next morning, Rebecca found footage from the one business with a camera in the alley behind Kyoto Dreams.

She immediately began to go through it, even though that meant holding off going through Diego Bosque's records. She couldn't remember ever having a case with so much data, but none of it pointing towards anything useful.

She was shocked to see the footage showed the same man with a San Francisco Giants baseball cap who had been at the two arson fires. He was skulking about on the corner, clearly watching what was happening at Kyoto Dreams. If he was there, did he kill Tanaka? Was he a murderer as well as an arsonist?

Once again, his baseball cap was worn so low, only his nose, mouth and chin were visible.

All this time, she'd had a niggling feeling as to who the arsonist might be. Now, an idea struck as to how she might prove it one way or the other: Facebook.

Anyone who worked as a writer probably had a Facebook page to promote his or her work. She typed in Connor Gray. Several men with that name came up. As she went through them, she found a match. Several links and comments about the *SF Beat* article were posted, as well as news stories on the arsons and murders.

But more interesting than any of that was Connor Gray's photos. She realized that chasing the man she saw at Big Caesar's had given her a better view of his face than any of the security cameras. The mysterious man hanging around the arson fires, and the alley behind Kyoto Dreams, was the writer of the tabloid article.

Now, the question was why.

She was pondering that when her once-upon-a-time-heart-throb, Inspector Paavo Smith, walked into Homicide. She was glad that she and Paavo were now friends with none of the uneasiness between them that her former crush had caused.

Instead of going straight to his desk, he stopped at Rebecca's and sat. "I haven't had a chance to talk to you alone since that tabloid article came out," he said. "Don't think too harshly of him."

He didn't have to mention Richie's name for her to know who he was talking about. She put down her pen. "I know the article was exaggerated. It's no big deal."

"Isn't it?" Paavo asked. "Angie told me what you said to her and Serefina. But I didn't believe it. And if the article is what is causing you to doubt him, you're making a mistake."

She was puzzled. "You were one of the many people warning me against Richie."

"I know, and I still want to make sure your eyes are open about him. That's one thing, but for you two to break up because of a lie is wrong."

She leaned back in her chair, arms folded and studied him. "And here I thought *I* was confused."

He smiled balefully. "I know, but all I can tell you, hearing everything third hand from his mother to Serefina to Angie to me, is that the guy is pretty darn serious about you. Also, Angie thinks he hangs the sun and the moon in the sky, which tells me a lot of good things about him. I just wanted you to know that."

Rebecca couldn't help but smile. Richie always called that kind of gossip "the Italian hotline," and he swore it could move faster than the speed of light. "Thank you for telling me, but I'm sure you've heard how badly stories get twisted when they go from one person to the next to the next." Rebecca turned more serious. "Who knows what Carmela really said? Besides, she hates me, and constantly worries that Richie *will* get serious about a cop who once 'got him shot' as she puts it. The way she blames me for a minor wound he got on his arm, you'd think he faced mortar fire and IAD rockets."

Paavo smiled and nodded. He, too, had gone through grief with the Amalfi's over falling in love with Angie. In his case, it was her father who would have loved to exile him to an island in the middle of nowhere. "No matter what Carmela says, Angie thinks the two of you are good for each other, and if nothing else, she's a good judge of such things."

"Angie scarcely knows me."

"But she knows Richie quite well, and she's always looking out for what's best for him."

Rebecca looked down at her desk, not able to meet Paavo's pale blue eyes as he spoke. She had seen how close everyone in Richie's family was. Since Richie had no siblings, and Angie and her four sisters had no brother, when they were little kids, Richie was like a big brother to Angie. As they got older, they all drifted apart, but for some reason, lately, they seemed to find each other again. She was glad—Richie needed stability in his life, and she even envied him the love the family surrounded him with, although she knew at times they could drive him half crazy. "I'm afraid, Paavo, as to what's best for him ... tell Angie, it isn't me."

"What's not you?"

Rebecca recognized that voice. She looked up to see Richie walking towards them and couldn't help but smile. She glanced back at Paavo who was now standing, and then she faced Richie again. *How much had he heard?* She wracked her brain, then answered, "I'm not one to bake cookies for a sale at Angie's church."

Richie's eyebrows rose, astonished. "Angie wanted you to bake cookies?" He pulled his ever-present wad of bills out of his pocket, took out two twenties and gave them to Paavo. "Tell Angie it's for the church. Better than cookies, I'm sure."

Paavo gaped at them both as he stood there with money suddenly in hand. "Uh, yeah. Thanks. Excuse me. I think I should go over to the jail." He hurried out of the bureau.

Richie frowned, then sat by Rebecca. "What was that all about?"

Rebecca shrugged. "You know Angie. So, what are you doing here?"

"Have you looked at the news this morning?"

"The news? Not yet. Why?"

"Moss Brannigan is the lead story. Word somehow got out that he's now a target of the 'serial killer' who's going after San Francisco's enticing bachelors."

She was shocked. "Serial killer? What serial killer?"

"Take a look." He pointed at her computer.

She went to some local news websites, and sure enough, there was Brannigan, surrounded by reporters, telling a tale of how someone tried to sabotage his cruiser.

"Brannigan claims his cruiser was tampered with," Richie said. "But it doesn't quite fit the murders, does it? Or the arsons."

His words puzzled her. "Are you thinking he might be lying?"

"I'm saying I'd like to take a look at his boat. I know something about them. I used to own a sailboat."

That was news. "You owned a sailboat? A little one, or was it large enough to go out on the Pacific?"

He smiled at her interest. "It was a good size. A thirty foot Cross trimaran. A real beauty. I hired a guy to sail it who knew what he was doing, of course. I never did get good enough to trust myself out on the Pacific without an expert with me. But I learned a lot about yacht-size boats before I finally bought one. I wanted one that could go a good distance. We went down the coast to Cabo San Lucas three times in it."

"That would be so much fun. Days and nights out on the ocean. I've only dreamed of doing such a thing."

He nodded and seemed to study her a moment. "She was a good ship. Once in a blue moon, I even miss her."

"I love how boats are female and have names. Moss Brannigan said he calls his the *Celine.* I think it's kind of creepy to name a boat after the woman who sang the theme song for the movie *Titanic.*"

He shrugged. "It's also a pretty name."

"Maybe. So, why did you sell your boat?"

"The upkeep on those things is ridiculous. They always need something done whether you use them or not. There's a saying among boaters, that your happiest day is when you buy a boat, and your next happiest is the day you sell it. I guess that sums it up pretty well."

She stood and put on her jacket. "Obviously Moss Brannigan hasn't had such a happy day as yet. We'll go see him, but keep in mind, a killer might be watching both of you, and seeing you together—"

"You worry too much, Mayfield." They went to the elevator, and he put his hands in his pockets as they waited. "It's too beautiful a day for anyone dying. And being stuck in an office is too close to it."

He had parked, as had become his habit, in the employee

parking area. She didn't know how he managed to get an employee parking pass, and frankly, she didn't want to know. He followed her to her apartment where she left her SUV and got into his Porsche 911 Turbo for the drive to the St. Francis Yacht Club. She figured her Ford Explorer would never get past the gate.

From the Club's parking lot, they walked along the marina to the piers. He stopped at one and stared at a boat there, *The Magic Flute.*

"That's where we used to dock the *Isabella,*" he said. "That boat is nice, but nothing like mine was."

Her smile faded. Isabella was his deceased fiancée's name. "Have you been down here since you sold it, or I guess I should say, her?" she asked.

"I've been to the area, but not out here on the piers." She watched the wind blow his hair as he looked out on the water. She let him gather his thoughts in silence. Finally he turned to her. "Let's see what the *Celine* is all about."

She took his arm, not sure why, but it felt right. They continued along the marina. "For all we know," she said, "Brannigan might have left already."

"And miss out on all this publicity?"

He was right. Up ahead they reached a small crowd of cameramen and reporters. In the center of them stood Moss Brannigan. Docked just a bit farther down the pier was his large, beautiful cruiser. "It's a plenty nice boat," Richie said. "A Marlow Mainship. I knew a guy who had one. I checked it out before deciding a sailboat was more my style. But I do remember something about the way it's designed makes it easy to work on, particularly to reach the engine and fuel and so on."

"What are you saying?"

"I'm not sure." He thought a moment. "Those babies hold a

lot of fuel—probably well over a hundred gallons. If he thought it was full, and it was nearly empty, where did the fuel go?"

"He said he noticed the fuel was missing after he was out on the Pacific a few hours. If a hole in the fuel line caused a slow leak, he wouldn't have seen the gas leakage."

Richie nodded, but didn't look convinced.

Rebecca dropped his arm as they neared Brannigan. "Mr. Brannigan," she called. "May we talk?"

He looked over at her and Richie.

"Hello, Moss," Richie called.

"Well, well. Inspector, Richie. What a surprise." He gave a smile to the reporters as he said, "I think we're finished here." He strolled over to Rebecca and Richie. "Maybe you'd like to come on board."

But a buzz went through the reporters as they recognized Richie. They then rushed towards him and stuck microphones in his face. "Are you here because you're also worried about attacks on the bachelors in the story?" one shouted.

He backed up. "I'm ... no. I'm just here to see my friend, Moss."

A cacophony of questions hit him as reporters and cameramen pushed and shoved to get closer.

A young reporter caught Rebecca's eye and held out her microphone. "Hello. Are you here with Richie Amalfi?"

Rebecca squared her shoulders. "I'm with the police department." That, she realized to her dismay, caused more questions to be shouted in her direction. She tried getting away from them. She wanted to talk to Brannigan, who had been left alone when the reporters charged Richie. But she didn't see him anywhere.

~

Richie answered the reporters' questions, doing his best to promote Big Caesar's as he did so, but all the while he searched for Brannigan. Finally, he saw him hurrying off the pier, and wondered what in the world was going on. First the guy asked them on board, and now he was practically running away from them. Brannigan seemed to be looking at his cell phone, and Richie couldn't help but wonder if he'd gotten some sort of important message on it.

Where was Rebecca? A reporter tossed another question his way. They were all the same, it seemed, and he could answer them with scarcely a thought. "No, I don't know why we're being targeted. No, nothing has happened to me or Big Caesar's since it was firebombed, and it's now re-opened and better than ever. Etc., etc."

Something felt wrong. He had no idea why, but the sudden need struck to find Rebecca and get away from there. It worried him that he couldn't see her—couldn't be sure she was all right.

He shifted a few steps in one direction and then the other, finally spotted her walking along the pier towards the *Celine*. Why, he wondered, would she be going onto the boat when Brannigan wasn't on it? Maybe she hadn't seen him leave the dock.

He turned around, his back to the reporters in order to get away from them. As he did, he noticed Brannigan standing in front of the yacht club, just staring out at his ship, an odd expression on his face.

Richie hurried along the pier Rebecca walked down.

"Rebecca!" he called. But she was too far away to hear him.

He started to run towards her.

Without warning of any kind, an ear-splitting blast filled the air. The *Celine* burst into a red-yellow-and orange ball of fire at the same moment as Richie saw Rebecca flung into the air like a rag doll and then land hard on a wooden pier several feet back from where she'd been. He wanted to run to her, but had to stop, to cover his eyes with his arm as ash, burning embers and more rained over the pier, other ships, and the water. A second blast followed the first, and the entire pier shook from the force of it.

He dropped his arm. Black smoke was all around. His eyes stung, and the acrid, burning smell of fire filled his nose and mouth. But none of that mattered.

Near the *Celine,* on the pier and not moving, lay Rebecca.

15

Rebecca felt someone's hands on her face, her arms. She forced her eyes open. The smoke was so heavy she could scarcely see, but she recognized Richie.

She ached all over, but she could feel the heat of the fire. She remembered the blast, the force of it lifting her off her feet. She remembered feeling as if she, like the *Celine,* was being torn apart, and then hitting the wooden pier so hard it knocked the breath out of her.

She could see that Richie was talking to her, but her ears were so painful, their ringing so loud, she couldn't begin to hear or respond. All she could think of was that they were in danger there—that they had to get away from the fire. She tried to sit up, and could see the relief on Richie's face. He quickly helped her and then put his arms around her and lifted her to her feet. Waiting a moment, to be sure nothing was broken and that she could walk, he held her tight and led her off the pier.

As they reached an area with less smoke, she saw reporters gawking in disbelief while their cameramen filmed the disaster. Richie had her lie down on a bench near the Yacht Club, and soon others who had been hit by falling debris, burned, or knocked to the ground by the blast, came to the same area. From there, she could see the flames and a tall plume of black smoke billowing up from what had once been Brannigan's cruiser.

Nearly all the injured had been on nearby boats or simply walking along the pier near the *Celine*. An emergency area was quickly set up, and the injured made to lie down, covered with blankets, until a doctor could see them. Rebecca didn't want to wait, but the manager of the yacht harbor and Richie refused to let her do anything until she was looked over.

Rebecca rubbed her ears, indicating to Richie what was wrong. He nodded. She didn't like how worried he looked.

"Moss ..." she said, finding it weird that, although she knew inside her head that she was talking aloud, she couldn't actually hear her own words. "He may have been on the boat."

Richie shook his head. She couldn't hear his answer, but his gestures told her Brannigan was away from the pier before the boat blew up.

She nodded.

If Rebecca thought the news media had gone crazy with its theories about some serial killer going after wealthy bachelors in San Francisco, it was nothing compared to the madness after the *Celine* blew up on live TV. Richie left her side only to stop her from being bothered by the reporters circling around both him and Moss Brannigan and as more and more media came to realize that not only had the boat blown up, but two of the remaining bachelors were present at the scene. In fact, several had heard Moss invite Richie onto his cruiser, and reported that two more of the "enticing bachelors" had been mere seconds away from a quick and horrifying death.

Soon, the paramedics arrived. They went first to those who were bleeding or burned.

"Here she is."

Rebecca hadn't realized that her hearing had been coming

back, or that the muffled roar she was hearing wasn't in her head, but actually was coming from the din of humanity around her. She'd been lying down with her eyes shut, but she opened them to see Richie and a man holding a doctor's bag. She blinked a few times and sat up.

"Can you hear me yet?" Richie asked.

"Yes—a little."

He looked relieved. "This is Doctor Levinfeld. He's a friend of mine. His house is just a couple of blocks away on Marina Boulevard, so I called, and fortunately, he was home and willing to come by to check you over."

Rebecca was speechless.

"Look this way, please," the doctor said, shining a light into her eyes and then spent a long time looking at her ears. He also listened to her heart, lungs, checked her balance, eye movements and so on, through the usual concussion protocol, then stood straight and said, "Miss Mayfield, you should be just fine. By tomorrow, the ringing in your ears should be gone completely. I see no sign of a concussion. There's a bump where your head hit the wooden pier a little too quickly, but it's not a concern. Be thankful you didn't land on concrete. A couple of Motrin and bed rest should make you feel good as new."

"Thank you, Doctor," she said.

Levinfeld shook hands with Richie who thanked him profusely for coming by so quickly. "It's all right. And since I'm here, I'll see if others need me. Anyway, it's good to see you worrying about someone besides yourself! Take care of her— and you, too, Richie. I hope the stories I'm hearing on the news are merely that—stories."

"I hope so as well," he said. Then the two said goodbye.

"I'm glad that's done. Thank you, Richie," Rebecca said, standing up. She put her hand in her pocket. "Oh, my God! My phone. It must have fallen out on the pier. I've got to try to find it. I must have been truly knocked silly if I didn't even miss it until now."

"It's okay. I've got it." He handed the phone to her.

Ten missed calls and frantic messages, all from Courtney. She called her back, putting the phone on speaker not wanting anything close to her sore ears.

"Where have you been?" Courtney cried. "I've been worried sick. You're all over the news!"

"I'm fine."

"Are you with Richie?"

"Yes, as a matter of fact."

"Let me talk to him."

Rebecca was surprised, but handed Richie the phone. His conversation consisted of a series of "yes" answers. Smart man. And then he said goodbye, ended the call, and handed the phone back to Rebecca. "She's with Pierre and is staying with him unless you need her."

"I don't," Rebecca said. "I'm going back to work."

"You're joking."

"Excuse me?"

"You've just been knocked half way to hell and back, and you're lucky your eardrums didn't burst. You need to go home to rest, and that's where I'm driving you."

She frowned. "A boat has just blown up."

"What, you're part of CSI now? Or maybe you're going to go scuba diving to see if you can find a detonation device? Forget it, Mayfield. Besides, all your potential victims are quite safe tonight—they're all being hounded by the press."

"Do you have anything at your house for dinner?" Richie asked.

"I'll find something," she muttered, not happy.

"There's a McDonald's up ahead. How about a Big Mac and fries—comfort food?"

Her unhappiness lessened. "Throw in a chocolate shake and it's a deal."

He bought enough for himself as well. As he headed towards Rebecca's apartment, he got a call from Tommy Ginnetti. He switched on the "hands-free" speaker. "Tommy, what's up?"

"People are already lining up to come inside," Tommy said excitedly.

"What do you mean? It's an hour before the club opens."

"I know! That's why I'm calling. I saw the news today, boss."

"Okay. I'll be there as soon as I can," Richie said. "I've got a couple things to do first."

"Actually, boss ... I think, for now at least, it'll be better if you aren't here."

"*What?*"

There was a long pause and then Tommy said, "I could be wrong, but maybe the club, rather than you, ought to be the center of attention tonight."

Richie was stunned until he thought about it a moment. "I suspect you're right," he said. "Keep me posted if there's any trouble."

"Will do."

Richie hung up. "Jeez, what a mess."

"Well, at least now you don't have to gobble down your dinner," Rebecca said as they reached Mulford Alley. She unlocked the doors and let him inside.

Richie had her sit on the sofa, feet up, while he put her dinner on a tray. He sat on a chair facing her with his food on the coffee table. He'd bought himself a vanilla shake as opposed to her chocolate one. Spike jumped onto the sofa and curled up beside Rebecca.

The two ate in silence, almost as if without talking they

could enjoy each other's company, but if one of them said something, no matter what, the other was sure to argue about it.

"That hit the spot," Richie said. "I guess I was more hungry than I thought."

"Me, too," Rebecca agreed. "And it does feel good to be home with Spike."

"Yeah, I guess so." He said nothing for a long while. "Listen, I want to tell you about that article—"

"You owe me no explanation," she said.

"I know. You 'couldn't care less.'" He used her words to him.

She shrugged and looked away. "It's not important."

"It's important to me." He waited until she looked back at him. "You've made it clear you think I'm no saint, but the love 'em and leave 'em story those two women told was bull."

"It doesn't—"

"Will you listen? One of them I dated twice and then realized we were all wrong. I never called her again. That's not love. And the other ... I met her, first date, at a coffee shop. We planned to have coffee and then go to a movie. I no sooner sat down than she asks, 'Can you see yourself married and a father by this time next year?' I swear, I drank that coffee down and got out of there so fast, I burned my mouth. I never did see the movie. And she's the one who cried when the reporter talked to her."

Rebecca tried hard not to laugh, she really did, but the image of Richie's reaction to his date's question got to her. He probably looked like his hair was on fire as he ran out of the place.

When he saw her smile, he did as well. "Scout's honor. It's all true."

She scooted as much as she could against the back of the sofa to make some room for him to sit beside her, then reached out her hand. He took it and sat facing her.

"I haven't told you yet, thank you for helping me today," she said. "I realized that while everyone else ran away from the boat, you ran towards it. You didn't know if the fire had already reached the gas tank, or if there might be another explosion and take the pier with it."

"It didn't."

"Still, it was a foolish thing for you to do."

"No." He brushed his fingertips lightly over the side of her face. "It wasn't."

She felt a pressure behind her eyes at his simple words, and at how completely undeserving she felt of them. She couldn't stop the feeling, nor could she stop how her heart filled just by looking into his dark eyes. She put a hand to his neck, then slid her fingers into his hair, to the back of his head, and pulled him toward her. "Richie ..."

She didn't have to say anything more.

16

Rebecca's phone buzzed. It was Courtney asking her to open the door. It was already nine in the morning. If Courtney stayed with her much longer, she was going to have to give her a key ... just as she'd given one to Richie.

Richie! Beside her, where Richie had been when she fell asleep, Spike now lay. He lifted his head to see what the disturbance was.

Rebecca put on her robe and slippers. Richie wasn't in the bedroom, bathroom or main room, which meant he wasn't in the apartment, and his clothes were gone. A part of her was glad not to have to face him this morning. They hadn't talked much last night—not about anything seriously, in any case. They'd just shown how much they had missed each other.

She went out and let in Courtney. "How do you put up with all this tension?" Courtney asked as they walked to the apartment. "I'd be a complete basket case!"

"But you had a nice time with Pierre, I take it," Rebecca said as she put on coffee.

"Yes, except he surely is nervous. Something's very wrong. I think he knows a lot more about Diego Bosque and Shig Tanaka than he's saying—and I don't think their deaths had anything to do with a tabloid article."

"Richie said much the same." As Rebecca made coffee, Courtney put her jacket and purse in the bedroom. When she came back out, she was grinning strangely.

"What?" Rebecca asked.

"Both sides of your bed were used last night, and it wasn't me. And the toilet seat was left up, and that wasn't you. I think Richie took even better care of you than he promised me he would."

Without a word, Rebecca put Courtney's coffee on the table and went off to take her morning shower.

Richie had woken up that morning as the sunlight began to fill Rebecca's bedroom. He sat up and looked at her peacefully sleeping. So much for his determination to have nothing more to do with her. She barely crooked her little finger and there he was.

He wondered what she would think of what had transpired between them. Yesterday, if she'd walked faster, if she'd been on that boat when it blew up, she would have been killed. That could be what had made her so emotional last evening, what had made her want to feel comfort and warmth from another person. Or, was it something more?

He knew he'd never forget how he felt as the blast knocked her a good five feet backwards, and when she'd landed so hard, and lay so still for what was probably seconds, but had seemed like hours.

The experience told him what he already knew about how he felt about her—and that it was crazy to feel that way. But as much as he cared, he couldn't know her mind.

He decided it was best to leave and to let her work out her feelings alone, and so he quietly dressed and left the apartment.

He wasn't normally up at this time of the morning and was surprised at how busy the streets were. He felt hungry, and thought of the one place he knew where he could get a good breakfast. He'd been remiss in not going there already since he'd gotten a stream of phone messages telling him how worried she was.

It was time to visit his mother.

Carmela Amalfi lived in a small flat near the top of Russian Hill, the same place she'd lived when Richie was growing up. He told her he would buy her a bigger house in a neighborhood that wasn't so crowded, but she refused to move, saying her friends were all nearby, and a bigger house meant more work to keep it clean. She refused any help along those lines. Once, Richie hired a cleaning lady for her. She would clean the house before the woman arrived (couldn't let some stranger think she lived in a dirty house, after all), and then Carmela redid most of the woman's work because she didn't find it up to her standards.

When Richie realized his mother was working twice as hard with a cleaning lady than without one, he let her go.

In any case, when the owner of the building put it up for sale a few years back, he bought it.

He let himself in the main door, and then up the stairs to the top flat. He unlocked her door. "Ma, you home?"

"Richie, finally! Where you been? I been so worried!" She was still in a robe and slippers, with no make-up, but not a hair on her head was out of place. He knew why. She had it styled each week, and the beautician put so much spray on it, a pith helmet would have more chance of being damaged. "Come in the kitchen. What are you doing up so early? Did you eat yet?"

He sat in his favorite chair at the kitchen table while she

poured him a cup of coffee. "Not yet. I got your messages and wanted to tell you I'm fine."

"I read that story about you! I was so upset!"

He'd expected that. "What's going on with the other guys in the article has nothing to do with me, okay. There's nothing for you to worry about."

She put several strips of bacon in a pan to cook. "What do you mean? I don't know about no other guys. What I want to know is, how come I never met any of your girlfriends? The ones in the story. You never told me you were so close to getting married. You should have let me know. I would have invited the girl to my house, cooked a nice dinner, maybe even some *mani-cott'*—your favorite, Richie. Why don't you tell me these things?"

He gaped. "I wasn't close—"

"Those women, they looked like nice girls. And they loved you so much. *Madon'*, I felt so sorry for them! And that one, the one who's still crying over you! *Poverina!* It broke my heart. I think there's a good chance she'll take you back. Especially if you apologize and tell her you made a mistake."

"I didn't make a mistake."

"To think, that they're still pining away. It made me weep for them, Richie!" She took a Kleenex from her bathrobe pocket and dabbed her still-dry eyes.

"Don't cry, Ma. Really." He tried to think of a way to get her off the subject. "How about I put on some toast while you fry the eggs?"

"All right." She sighed. "I'm happy to cook for my still-single son because he doesn't have a wife to cook a big breakfast for him and all your kids."

He rolled his eyes. He thought she was upset about the deaths and arsons. He should have known better. He got up and put bread in the toaster and then took the butter and raspberry jam from the refrigerator. "In case you see me or Rebecca on the news next to a boat that blew up, she's fine."

"I already saw the story." Carmela tightened her lips. "It was bad enough she got you shot, now she takes you places where things explode. And you wonder why I think you need to go back to those nice, safe women who loved you so!" She cracked one egg so hard the shell shattered into a bunch of little pieces that fell into the pan, sticking to the egg white. "*Ma che fai!* See what you made me do!" She scooped up the whole egg and threw it away.

"It was a nice boat, before it blew," Richie said, deciding to ignore the egg fiasco. "It made me think I was wrong to sell my sailboat. I might get another one. Or even a cabin cruiser."

"Those cabin cruisers, they have an engine? So you don't have to worry about the wind all the time? It used to make me sick, you out in the ocean, depending on a big sheet to get you home again."

"It wasn't a sheet," he said, but quickly realized that was a losing argument. "What I liked about the cruiser I saw was that if anything goes wrong, it's relatively easy to fix ..." He thought about the way the boat was set up, how accessible the engine was in case there was a problem at sea. And how an old tar and tour boat operator like Moss Brannigan had to know a lot about how such a boat operated. How could he not have known the boat was leaking fuel at a massive rate until he was so far from San Francisco that he felt his life was in danger? It didn't make sense for a man like him.

And how was it that the boat blew up during the exact moment when he—and everyone else—were far enough away from it that no one was killed? Yes, Rebecca was going towards it, but at least it exploded before she was in danger. Almost as if ...

What kind of detonation device had been used? And who

would profit the most from blowing up what was surely a well-insured money pit?

He had to talk to Shay. He stood. "I've got to get going."

Carmela had already put the bacon on a plate and was just now adding the eggs. "You sit! I made this for you, and you're going to eat. Maybe you don't get enough good food and that's why you're so *patz'* that you don't find a good woman to marry." She put the plate in front of him with a thud. "At least I'm glad it's over between you and the cop."

Her last words struck deep. He sat back down. "What do you mean?"

"It's over. She told Angie and Serefina you two were *finito*. It's about time. *Mangia!*"

Rebecca must have talked to them while she was mad at him. Maybe after their steak dinner blow-up. Had she meant it then, or had she meant it last night?

He took out his cell phone and went to the liar app. He clicked on the information about Rebecca.

From what the app was telling him, the woman never told the truth at all.

17

Homicide's secretary, Elizabeth, made a breathless call to Rebecca's desk to tell her a "Mr. Fontaine" was waiting for her in reception. When Rebecca went to meet Pierre, she found Elizabeth was gawking at him as if she'd been dumbstruck with love.

"Thank you," Rebecca said to her. The secretary made no response. "Pierre, let's go to my desk."

Inspectors Calderon and Benson were in the bureau, and both suddenly grew quiet as Rebecca entered with the hotelier. Pierre sat in the guest chair at her desk, but looked decidedly uncomfortable.

"What is it?" Rebecca asked.

He looked around. "Maybe ... not here," he whispered.

"Let's go to an interview room." She made a face at the eavesdroppers as she led Pierre into a dingy green room with a single table and a one-way mirror. They sat facing each other on opposite sides of the table.

The lines on Pierre Fontaine's face seemed deeper, more careworn. He inhaled a deep breath. "I was supposed to meet

Courtney at eleven for brunch. It's now one, and I haven't heard from her and can't reach her on her cell."

Rebecca wasn't sure how to react. "Courtney does lose track of time easily." She was trying to assure herself as well as Pierre. "It's probably nothing."

"Yes, but she was going to Diego Bosque's store. Last night, we were talking about the clothes there, and she grew quite excited about something. She planned to go there and talk to the store manager around ten."

Rebecca drew in her breath. "Ten," she repeated; three hours earlier. "And then she planned to meet you afterward?"

"That's right. When it got to be noon, I called Easy Street. People are there working, moving all the old clothes out, and cleaning. The manager, Peters, I think his name is, said she'd been there. He swore she left around ten-thirty, in plenty of time to meet me. I tried waiting, but now, I'm worried, and so I came here."

Her lips tightened. "Okay. We will need to go back out to my desk."

Pierre rushed to keep up with her.

"Bo, Luis," she called the other inspectors. "We've got to find my sister. Here's her cell phone number. See if one of you can find it. She's driving a rental car. Budget. I'll call them and get the license plate number and see if we can track it. She was last seen at Easy Street Clothiers. She was meeting the manager, Dan Peters, at ten this morning. He said she left around ten-thirty. She might show up on traffic cams. They cover that down-town-Financial district area pretty well."

Inspectors Benson and Calderon didn't say a word, but went straight to work. When a relative of one of their own was in danger, that took precedence over everything else going on. While Bo worked to get a GPS signal from Courtney's phone,

Calderon tapped into the traffic cameras around Easy Street to see if he could find any signs of Courtney.

It took little time to discover that her cell phone had either been turned off or was destroyed. It was sending no GPS signal.

Rebecca managed to quickly get a license plate for a white Ford Focus.

Calderon had no luck searching for a woman who looked somewhat like Rebecca but with red hair. They all crowded around the traffic camera feed looking for the rental car. After about ten minutes, they found it parked some four blocks from the store. Ironically, it had several traffic tickets gracing its windshield for staying overtime at a parking meter.

"Go back to Easy Street," Rebecca said. "Let's look for her leaving the store."

"It's in the middle of the block, so the traffic cams don't pick it up directly," Calderon explained.

They carefully watched the corners surrounding the clothier, hoping to see her crossing one of them. There was nothing. "Look at that," Rebecca said, pointing to a white van that was seen crossing an intersection towards the clothier. A couple of minutes passed before they saw the same van at the next intersection. "It doesn't take that long to go from one corner to the next," Rebecca said. "And if it stopped to make a pickup or delivery, it should have taken longer than two minutes."

Calderon shook his head. "It could be anything. Maybe the van had to wait for someone who was parking. Who knows?"

"Can we get a license plate off it?"

Benson zoomed in and then read it off to Rebecca who logged into the California DMV system. "We've got a problem," she said, her voice hushed.

"What is it?" Benson asked.

Rebecca stared at the screen, doing her best not to let anyone see how upset this had made her. "The license plate is off a stolen ten-year-old green Ford Ranger. It doesn't belong with the white van at all. Someone in that van might have taken her."

"*Merde,*" Pierre muttered.

"Pierre, go back to your hotel. Courtney might try to reach you there. I'm heading to Easy Street to talk to Dan Peters."

"I shall come with you," Pierre said.

"Not a good idea," she told him firmly.

He didn't argue.

"I'll talk to store owners in the area," Calderon said. "Someone may have seen something."

"I'll do what I can to track the white van on the traffic cams," Benson said. "If it doesn't work, I'll join Luis canvassing the area."

"Thank you," Rebecca said as her gaze went to her two coworkers and to Pierre. "All of you."

Then they left.

Rebecca was about to get into her SUV when her phone rang. To her surprise, it was Shay.

"What's up?" she asked, knowing Shay would never phone for no reason.

"Have you heard from Richie or your sister over the past couple of hours?" he asked.

Her breath caught. "I'm trying to find my sister right now. I don't know where she is. Why? What's going on?"

"Richie and I were supposed to work on some, uh, business around noon. He said he had to meet your sister first. He seemed to think the meeting wouldn't take long, but now he's over an hour late, and I can't reach him. I was wondering if you knew what was going on."

"This makes no sense," Rebecca said. "If she was in trouble, why call Richie and not me?"

"Maybe it depends on who she's in trouble with," Shay suggested.

Rebecca told him about Pierre Fontaine's visit. Shay didn't like it at all and without another word, hung up the phone.

She wasn't sure what to make of that, but had only gone one block when he sent her a text. He'd located Richie's Porsche in the Mission district.

She guessed he decided not to waste time asking if she'd join him there. He knew she would.

The area was named for Mission Dolores, one of the original California missions built long before the land ever became a state. It was home to a large Mexican and Central American population, and although in the very heart of the city and a regular target for urban renewal projects, it remained an area of mostly small, run-down homes and high crime. It wasn't the sort of area in which Richie would ever leave his beloved Porsche out on the street.

It couldn't have stood out more if it had neon lights on it.

She pulled into a loading zone, and Shay showed up almost immediately and parked behind her. He drove a black Maserati. The neighbors were probably having palpitations, assuming a bigwig gang meeting of some kind was going on. The two of them looked around, but saw nothing that gave any idea where Richie might be.

A pharmacy was on the corner, across the street from the Porsche. Inside, Rebecca showed her badge.

"Do you have outside security cameras?" she asked. "I'd like to see them."

The pharmacist looked like he was going to protest when Shay quietly said, "Right now." Something about a man who wore an expensive tan cashmere jacket, a white shirt, and Kelly green silk ascot, while coldly and fiercely making a demand, was so off-putting and bizarre, it caused people to not even consider crossing him.

The pharmacist brought them into the back room. The surveillance system was digital, and Shay was able to get it to work in no time flat. They saw the two men walk up to Richie as he got out of his Porsche. Just the way they held their hands Rebecca knew they were armed. They walked him to a Mercedes and put him in it. The license plate was clearly shown.

Rebecca got on the phone to Homicide and told Bo Benson what was going on. He ran the plate number for her. Of course, it came up as belonging on a VW bug. But the photo she sent of one of the men with Richie matched a facial recognition criminal records file.

"Uh oh," Benson said. "Mariano Cepeda. He's got an arrest record a mile long. He's a big shot in the Thirteens. There's an address on record, but who knows." He gave her the address.

Her heart sank. The 13's were ruthless and deadly. The thought of both Courtney and Richie being in their hands ...

Rebecca remembered that the cop she had been dating before Richie had worked the beat involving the 13's, a Mexican drug-running gang. If anyone knew where the 13's might hide someone they'd snatched, it was Ray Torres. She gave him a call.

"Rebecca, it's good to hear your voice again," Torres said. His voice was low, soft, and hopeful. She felt kind of bad that she'd made him unhappy when she stopped seeing him. He was a good man, and he was going to make some lucky woman very happy. But she wasn't that woman. "How have you been?"

"Not too bad, Ray. I'm calling about a case."

"Ah. I see." His disappointment was clear.

"Someone involved in a murder investigation has been picked up by Mariano Cepeda and another man. We think they're bringing him somewhere to be questioned. Do you have any idea where that might be?"

"If they're bringing him to meet the head of the Thirteens, you don't want to mess with him. Cepeda is his main man, but believe me, he's bad news."

"I'm sure he is." Her voice turned cold. "What can you tell me?"

"It's your funeral. His name is Gonzalo Piña. They call him El Grande. You'll find him on Twenty-Ninth Street, near Dolores." He didn't have the number, but he gave her a description of the house.

As Rebecca drove, she explained to Shay that the 13's were a local drug gang connected with the Norteños. They constantly battled with the Sureños from Los Angeles to maintain their hold on drug trafficking in the city. They easily found the house that Ray Torres had described. Parked directly in front of it was the Mercedes from the security video.

She parked around the corner and then handed Shay a bullet-proof vest before putting one on herself. She always carried a spare in her SUV because her partner, Sutter, so often forgot his—as if, without a vest, he had an excuse to stay away from dangerous situations. Then, ready to go, her heart pounding at what they might find, she and Shay crept towards the house.

Rebecca crouched in shadows near the front steps while Shay took the handle of his gun and smashed in the Mercedes' driver's side window. He then joined Rebecca as the car alarm erupted in a shrill wail.

The door to the house burst open and two men with guns came running out and down the four front steps to the sidewalk. Rebecca tripped one as he ran by and hit him on the back of the head with the butt of her gun as he fell. He landed unconscious on the sidewalk. At the same time, Shay gave the other an upper cut punch to the chin that stunned and spun him, followed by a knuckle to the temple that laid him flat.

Rebecca and Shay ran to the landing for the front door and stood with their backs plastered to the wall on each side of it and waited. Her mouth dry, Rebecca wondered if their plan had any chance of working at all, when a third man came through the doorway, scratching his stomach and bellowing about the Mercedes still shrieking. Rebecca plunged the back of her upper arm hard into his windpipe. Stunned, he bent forward, gasping, and unable to breathe or cry out. She slammed her elbow into a pressure point behind his ear. He dropped, out cold.

Shay gave a quick, congratulatory nod, and Rebecca allowed herself a small smile as they entered the house, guns drawn, knowing they had to move fast.

Voices came from down the hall. Rebecca crept forward and peered around a moldy doorframe. She saw Richie in a chair, the side of his face with a dark red welt. Two men stood over him. One was short, thin, and very young, with a long, stringy mustache and goatee, and scraggly long black hair. The other was heavy, and older. He wore expensive-looking clothes and a massive gold watch that matched his gold front tooth. His face had a scar from cheek to chin that all but danced as he swore a blue streak in Spanish.

Her eyes searched for her sister, and found her sitting on the floor against a side wall, her ankles and mouth duct-taped, and her arms pulled behind her back as if they, too, were taped together. Courtney's eyes were wide, terrified, and her face was tear-streaked. Fury filled Rebecca, and the thought flashed that if she weren't a cop, she might just shoot the bastards that did this to people she loved and cared about.

Shay, she knew, didn't have such qualms. She met his gaze and gestured that she was going in. He gave her a thumbs up.

With her gun held at eye level, aimed at El Grande's chest, she stepped into the kitchen. "Police. Let them go! Now!"

But the young fellow drew his gun.

"Put it down!" she yelled.

He didn't, and Shay fired, hitting the hand of the gunman. The gun flew into the air, while the bullet apparently kept going and ended up in his shoulder, knocking him to the ground. He held his shoulder, writhing and crying in pain.

"Don't try it!" Rebecca warned, turning her gun back on the scar-faced man who was just then reaching behind his waist.

He froze, then put his hands up. "Get out of here," he said to Richie. "Just remember what I told you."

Richie nodded at him and went to Rebecca's side. While Rebecca held the gun on El Grande and his still-whimpering companion, Shay cut the tape off Courtney and lifted her to her feet.

Rebecca took the lead to be sure no surprises waited for them outside, followed by Richie, Courtney, and then Shay, who walked backwards to keep his eyes on the men in the kitchen.

Once out of the house, they hurried to Rebecca's car and drove away before El Grande called for help.

"Are you okay?" she asked Richie and Courtney as she drove.

"I am, thanks to Richie coming when I called. They made me do it, Rebecca." Courtney's tears flowed.

"Richie?" Rebecca asked.

"Yeah, fine." He sounded angry.

"Thank you so much for helping Courtney," she told him.

He nodded, but still seemed in no mood to talk.

But Courtney was. "It's drugs and money laundering," she said. "I recognized the clothes connection from a similar drug money laundering scheme in the Los Angeles fashion district. It's been stopped, but it was one of the biggest in the country, and run by the Sureños gang. I went to Easy Street and talked to

Dan Peters, the manager. He didn't seem to know anything, but clearly the place is being watched because when I left, a couple of guys grabbed me and put me in the back of a van. I was brought to a house and asked what I know. But I know nothing! They insisted Richie knew, and that I should call him and ask to meet. I ... I did."

"You didn't try to warn him?" Rebecca asked with a fierce scowl.

"How?" Courtney wailed, then scrunched down a little in the car seat. "They're scary guys, Rebecca. Really scary."

Rebecca said nothing more to her as she reached the street where Richie's and Shay's cars were, miraculously, still there waiting. She parked and, while Courtney stayed in the car, she got out with Richie and Shay. Other than the bruise, Richie seemed okay. She would have said something about it, but he didn't look in the mood to hear any sympathy. He'd been picked up by thugs, punched, and was furious. She got it.

She walked with him to his car. Richie faced her. "El Grande seems to think you know more about what's going on than you do," he said once he stopped clenching his teeth. "Your sister started asking questions in Easy Street Clothiers that got back to him somehow and apparently pushed all his paranoid buttons. I tried to explain she was a reporter from Los Angeles and knows nothing about what goes on in this city. I said he needed to let her go unless he wanted a lot more trouble. You don't take on a cop's family with impunity."

"How did he capture you?"

"I was stupid. I knew something weird was going on when I got Courtney's call, since it came by way of Big Caesar's. That told me it had nothing to do with you. I thought—assumed— she wanted to talk about Pierre. It wouldn't be the first time one of his women called, wanting to know if he had a wife or girl-friend hidden away, or if she had any chance at all with him.

Anyway, Courtney sounded upset, so I agreed to meet her. El Grande's men, not Courtney, waited for me."

"I can't believe she'd make a call that would put you in danger that way!"

"Believe me, she did what any normal person would do when being threatened and coerced by men like that," Richie said. "She's not a cop, Rebecca."

"I guess."

"I'll admit, El Grande's worse than I imagined. I thought he'd be more reasonable, at least able to listen. Unfortunately, he was neither."

"What do you mean?" she asked.

"He thought I was involved with things I'm not."

"Like what?"

"Everything. Apparently, there's a war going on. It's stayed under the police radar, but it's happening. Somebody powerful is trying to move into the city. Their fingers are in all kinds of things—especially drugs and money laundering, like Courtney said. For some reason, that guy, El Grande, thinks I know who these newcomers are. I kept telling him I have no idea what he's talking about, but he said everyone told him otherwise. I know my reputation, and sometimes I really hate it." And he looked straight at Rebecca as he added, "In all kinds of areas."

She looked at Shay as well as Richie. "Should we all meet somewhere? Talk about this?"

"No. Not now," Richie said. "I'm going home. And you have a sister to take care of."

She couldn't help but suspect Shay would go with Richie to talk in more detail about what had happened. But he was right, she was needed elsewhere.

18

———————

Rebecca drove Courtney to her rental car, and its parking tickets, and then they met at her apartment.

Once inside, tears again filled Courtney's eyes. "I'm so sorry! I didn't expect any trouble, and I never expected to put anyone in danger."

"It's not your fault, Courtney," Rebecca said.

She dried her eyes as best she could. "I also see, with the constant danger around this kind of work, it's not for me. I don't want to do news. I don't want to think about, let alone see, heads without bodies, boats blown up, and scary gang leaders threatening to slice off my ears and fingers until I tell them things I don't even know!" She shuddered. "I'm going back to L.A. I'll head to the airport now."

"I'm so sorry it turned out this way," Rebecca said. "Will you see Pierre before you go?"

"No. I'll send him a text, explaining it all."

"I see."

"He'll understand. Believe me."

Rebecca understood as well, even as she realized she was

surprisingly sorry to see her sister leave. "Take care of yourself, Courtney."

"You, too. Be careful! And take care of Richie. He's my hero. You two ... maybe you aren't quite as different as you think."

They gave each other a hug and a quick kiss on the cheek, and then Courtney hurried out the door.

~

"There she is. Finally!" Carmela Amalfi said to her friend, Geraldine Vaccarino. The two women sat side-by-side on "guest chairs" at Rebecca's desk.

Rebecca froze just inside Homicide's doorway, stunned to see them there. After all the emotion and the fear and the potentially deadly gunfight she'd just faced, Richie's mother was the last person in the world that she wanted to see. She was tempted to cut and run, but Carmela was already giving her a little wave.

She had met Carmela a few times and had met her friend Geri during a case involving Geri's deceased sister. The only other person in the room was a sheepish Paavo Smith, who quickly gathered some papers, his jacket and gun.

"You're in good hands now," he said a little too cheerfully to Carmela, his wife's aunt. "I have to get going." He gave Rebecca an apologetic glance as he dashed past her to the elevator. "They've been waiting about an hour." She was sure he felt every one of the daggers her eyes shot at him.

"He's a good man, that Paavo," Carmela said to Geri, watching Paavo disappear into the hallway. "My niece, Angie, did okay, I guess."

"Handsome, too. And big. I do like a big man," Geri said and the two ladies chortled.

"Carmela, Geri," Rebecca interrupted as she reached her

desk. She didn't even try to smile. Or sound particularly civil. "I'm sorry you had to wait. No one told me you were here."

"I thought you'd be here sooner," Carmela said. "I hear how you're always working when you've got a case, and I know you have a big one since *my son is in danger*."

Rebecca sat. "I'm trying to make sure he understands the danger as well."

"Good." Carmela squared her shoulders. "I heard you and Richie don't see each other anymore. I want to make sure that won't get in the way of you working this case."

Rebecca might have been insulted, but she understood Carmela better than that. "It won't."

"*Bene.* Also, we want to help," Carmela said. "If there's anything we can do..."

Geri chimed in. "We were pretty good not so long ago."

"Yes, you both were." Rebecca still had nightmares over the dangers those women once faced, whether they realized it or not. She didn't want to think about Richie's reaction if anything had happened to them. "I don't think there's anything you can do at the moment. But thank you, and I'll keep you in mind."

"Richie shouldn't be alone," Carmela said.

Rebecca's mouth dropped, wondering what Carmela could possibly be suggesting.

"You should insist he stay at my house," Carmela said. "He'll be fine there. He won't listen to me, but if *the police* were to tell him to move in with his mother until the danger passes ..." She gave Rebecca a steel-eyed stare.

Rebecca once saw Richie's old room in his mother's flat. It looked like a shrine—his toys were still in it. She could just imagine him trying to live there now. "I certainly can suggest it," she said. And then some devilish impulse took over and Rebecca couldn't help herself. "Or, maybe he needs someone to stay with him. As protection. A bodyguard. In fact, maybe *I'm the one* who should—"

"No. I'm sure that won't be necessary." Carmela stood, and then Geri did the same. "Just make sure you keep him alive by finding the killer."

"You know," Geri said to Carmela, "the girl does have a point about staying with Richie. I mean, she carries a gun and all."

"*Statagitt'!*" Carmela said under her breath to Geri. Of course, it wasn't as if Rebecca could understand her, although she imagined "shut up" would be a good guess. Ironically, from what Richie had told her about the Calabrese dialect Carmela spoke, not many Italians would have understood her either.

"We're going." Carmela eyed Rebecca. "I hope you find whoever is trying to hurt Richie right away. I don't like having to worry about him. Although, come to think of it, I always do."

"Goodbye, Rebecca," Geri said.

Carmela waved.

"*Ciao!*" Rebecca called and couldn't help but chuckle to herself as she watched Carmela cringe.

19

———————

The crime scene unit's forensic report on the explosion on Moss Brannigan's cruiser was hand-carried to Rebecca's desk. Plastique, apparently near the engine, had been set off by a cell phone signal. Her eyes narrowed. That might have explained how it exploded when no one was so close they might have been killed. But it didn't tell her who did it. Or why.

She was pondering those questions when she heard footsteps approaching her desk and looked up.

"Richie." She felt as if she'd become a stop on the Italian hotline with all the visitors she was getting.

He looked one way and then the other. "Nobody else is here," he said and then leaned forward to give her a brief kiss, then a longer one.

And, since no one was there, she stood and kissed him back. "I was so worried about you."

"I was hoping Shay would contact you when I missed our meeting. Still, when you and he came in all armed and danger-ous, it was great. What badasses!"

"Good." She kissed him again, glad for once to be at her desk alone. "So," she sat down. "What brings you here? I thought you were going home to rest after all that."

"I did, for a while. But first I wanted to thank you for getting me out of there in one piece, and also to give you some information."

"What information?"

"I kept thinking about the story Moss Brannigan told you about losing gas on his yacht. It just didn't make sense to me. Not that I know much about boating, but I do know B.S. And Brannigan knows a lot about boating. Anyway, I asked Shay looked into Brannigan's financials.

"The guy was about to lose his business. The *Celine* was a huge money pit for him. It was having some problems that routine maintenance should have taken care of, but it seems he didn't have the money to do it timely, so the little problems grew into big, expensive ones. In fact, he couldn't even sell the boat in the shape it was in. I kind of doubt he ever took it under the Golden Gate—that water's really rough—let alone all the way up to Mendocino. A lot of his problems would be solved if the yacht just went away, and he got money from his insurer. I think, between the arson fires and then the murderer, he saw an opportunity and took it."

"You're suggesting he blew up his own boat?"

"It would make sense."

She agreed. Something about Brannigan's showboating at the Central Station, and the way he all but called a press conference over his "bachelor" troubles hadn't sat well with her. "It fits," she said. "Especially since the bomb was apparently triggered by a cell phone. We'll get on it with that in mind."

"Good." He leaned back and folded his hands behind his head, elbows out. "Any time you want a case solved ..."

"Thank you, Mr. Holmes. By the way, my sister went back to L.A."

"I'm not surprised. El Grande is going to give her nightmares for a long time, I'm afraid."

"I would have hoped Pierre Fontaine could keep away bad dreams."

He shook his head. "Courtney knows better than that. Pierre's the type of guy who'll wait until he's around fifty and then marry a twenty-two-year-old airhead with a lot of money."

She found it interesting that he knew Courtney would recognize that about Pierre, and she hadn't. She then told him about Carmela's visit to her. "So, basically, I've met everyone except the elusive Logan Travis and the writer of the article, Connor Gray. He's the one who was watching the arson fires, and I suspect he's the one who set them as well. I had been thinking that whoever set the fires also committed the murders and blew up Brannigan's yacht, but that doesn't make sense. I think I've been looking at this all wrong."

"How so?" Richie asked.

"First, let's ignore Brannigan. He's not involved except to use the 'bachelor' troubles to rid himself of an albatross. That leaves us with arsons and murders. The arsons were unprofessional, and would have only done damage to buildings if it weren't for the unfortunate fellow who died in a fire. The murders were horrific, cold and ugly. Doesn't sound, to me, like the actions of the same person."

"You're right," Richie said. "But I'm sure Logan Travis doesn't know anything. Trust me on that. But Connor Gray is another story. You know, he threw all kinds of hints in his write-up about something shady going on. I thought it was just to sell magazines, but what if he had actually stumbled across something?"

"That could be," Rebecca said. "Liv Wong said he was really excited about the story. He thought it might sell a lot of copies if she could get enough publicity. Unfortunately, her budget simply doesn't allow that."

He thought a moment. "But what about free publicity? Just like the six of us had wanted?"

"Arson fires. Of course!" Rebecca shook her head in disgust. "Didn't I say arsonists like to look at their handiwork?"

"Two arson fires within two days had already caused the *Chronicle* and other reports to link them to the *SF Beat* story," Richie said. "What if there were six fires? That would have meant big publicity for the little schmuck."

"And planning to set six fires would explain why Connor Gray went skulking around, watching all of you. That would explain why he was caught on camera sneaking around the alley behind Kyoto Dreams." Her eyes widened. "What if, when he was there, he saw the murder? And the murderer? What if that's why he's missing?"

"In other words," Richie said, "if he saw who killed Shig, he may be dead as well."

She nodded. "Let me call Eastwood and get an authorization to put out an APB on him."

He waited while she explained to her boss what was happening and why the all-points bulletin was necessary. She got his okay and then sent out the alert along with the driver's license photo and one from Connor Gray's Facebook page. "Now, we wait," she said when that was taken care of.

"No. Now you send all the information on Easy Street and Kyoto Dreams to Shay. I'll fill him in on it. There are a few things I've got to take care of tonight."

A cold chill went through her. "Not anything involving El Grande, I hope."

He hesitated, then said only, "Not directly."

He gave her a quick goodbye kiss and left.

She tried not to think about what he was up to and turned instead to gathering information to send to Shay.

20

———————

Rebecca had worried about Richie all night after hearing him say he was going after El Grande, directly or not. She hoped she had misunderstood him. By the next afternoon, she had an excuse to call him and to see how he was doing.

A bit earlier, she had found Logan Travis at the sandwich shop eating his tuna salad on rye, just as her sister had predicted. She followed him home. She knew she could knock on his door, and bully her way inside to question him, but from all she'd heard the man would probably just clam up.

Instead, she phoned Richie and told him she wanted to have him meet her at Travis's home so she could question him. Richie insisted he talk to Travis first, to smooth the way. She insisted he do so immediately—especially since she was sitting in her car, a half-block from his client's front door.

Ten minutes later, Richie called back to say Logan Travis was willing to talk to her, as long as Richie was also present. She agreed.

～

"What can I help you with?" Travis asked as she and Richie sat in his living room.

"You mentioned that you had someone lurking around your house," Rebecca said. "Do you have any videos or other information on him?"

"I have some old videos saved," Travis said. "But the lurker hasn't been back for some time." He led them to a room filled with computer monitors, servers, and drives. He typed in a few words, and in a few seconds, a black-and-white screen opened up, and a man in a hoodie was seen creeping through the garden. "That's the same man I saw at your home," Rebecca said to Richie.

Richie nodded then faced Travis. "My security cameras couldn't get his face. Did yours have any luck?"

"Let's see." Travis had a bunch of cameras in various positions. He went through several streams until he finally found one that showed more of an outline of the man's face than most. "I can run it through facial recognition software, once I'm into the California DMV files. It's going to take time to run, however. I've got to keep the breach low level so they don't know they've been hacked."

"Why don't you give this a try first?" Rebecca said and, using her phone, showed him the APB information she'd sent out.

Travis fed the photo into his system and ran a facial scan. As she was sure it would, it matched. Connor Gray obviously liked hiding his face under hoodies as well as baseball caps.

"We've got to find him," Rebecca said.

"I can do that," Travis announced.

Rebecca faced him. "You can?"

"Since he was here, my system synced with his phone. It's another app I've designed, along with the liar app you're testing, Richie."

"Liar app?" Rebecca repeated, looking at Richie.

He didn't look back. "Tell me about your design, Logan."

"Sure. It lets you sync to anyone's phone who comes close to you or your property. You can get into their GPS system as well as their mail and text messages."

Rebecca was stunned. "Do you know how completely illegal that is?"

Travis shrugged. "If someone comes onto my property uninvited, he deserves to have his privacy compromised."

She gave him a sideways glance, but didn't argue the point. "Okay, what did you find?"

"First, let me explain that I only did this to be sure he wouldn't come back and get near me. If he had, my phone would have signaled an alarm. But if you just want to know where he is, that's child's play."

He opened another program and soon located Connor Gray's phone. Its signal was coming from a spot a bit past Inverness, a small town on the western side of Tomales Bay, off Marin County's Sir Francis Drake Boulevard.

"Let's go get him," Rebecca said.

Richie nodded, then looked at his client. "You don't want to come along, or do you?"

"Hell, no. I want nothing to do with him."

"Okay, the Inspector and I will take it from here, but first one thing." Richie faced him straight on.

Travis waited. "Yes?"

"I'm assuming you synced my phone as well as the Inspector's to your damned system. Right now, you keep an eye on it in case we get into trouble. If we do, you call this number." He handed Travis a card with no name, but one of Shay's numerous cell phone numbers on it.

"Will do," Travis said, pocketing the card.

"Good. And then, once I call and tell you that everything's fine, you'll have five minutes to take our phones off your system. Understand? Five minutes, or your whole set-up here turns into nothing more than metallic Tinker toys."

Travis scoffed. "You forget, I've got a high-level security set up."

"And who got it for you?" Richie asked.

Travis's face fell and his lips formed a big "Oh."

Richie drove across the Golden Gate Bridge to Sir Francis Drake Boulevard and followed it westward. Rebecca had always loved this drive past the north side of Mount Tamalpais into a beautiful green wonderland that was filled with mostly dairies and ranch land. She had been out here a few times previously to visit a cheese factory and to go to Tomales Bay for crab and oysters.

The GPS signal Travis had set up led them past Inverness, and then onto Pierce Point Road towards the ocean.

As they passed a small dirt road, the signal began to lessen. They turned back to the dirt road and stopped. There was no way Richie's low-riding Porsche could drive up it.

"See, I told you my SUV had its uses," Rebecca said.

"Once in a blue moon, I'll agree." He slowly, carefully drove only far enough that the Porsche wouldn't be visible from the main road. Even that short distance over rocks and ruts had made him wince.

They got out of the car to a hilly land filled with redwood trees and thick brush. Richie was amazed that he still had a cell signal. He figured it was only because a lot of computer tech people had built luxurious second homes along the ocean front, not far from here.

It was actually good that they had to walk because if driving, they probably would have missed the tire tracks that turned onto what was essentially a deer path. After about five minutes, they saw an old beige Volvo stopped up ahead of them. Rebecca took out her Glock and insisted Richie walk behind her.

"Remind me to buy bullet-proof vests to keep in my car the way you do," Richie muttered. "One for each of us. I'm tired of getting in these situations and then having you out in front, with no protection except your gun."

"Hopefully, I won't need the gun," Rebecca said, but she just wasn't sure what she was going to find, or what Connor Gray's reaction to seeing them would be.

No one was in or near the Volvo. They kept going, looking for any hint that Connor was still out here.

Richie was the first to notice a building on the downslope of the hill. They found a footpath through the thicket and walked down it as quietly as they could until they arrived at a weathered, barely standing, one-room shack.

They reached a window and peered inside. It was empty.

"Drop the gun!" a voice called from some distance away.

They turned. High on the hill, all but hidden by trees and high weeds, Connor Gray stood aiming a rifle at them.

Rebecca carefully lowered her weapon to the ground.

"We came here to talk to you," Richie shouted. "We think you're in danger."

"In danger from you!" Connor answered.

"You're in much worse danger than from us," Rebecca called. "We want to help you, and to stop this."

"Connor," Richie said, "you know who I am, so you know I'm in danger, too. I think you know a lot about what's going on. We need to help each other."

Connor didn't reply.

Rebecca spoke. "I believe you had no idea a homeless man was sleeping inside when you set the fire at Easy Street."

"I didn't set anything!" Connor cried.

"I saw you there. Also at Big Caesar's, and at Kyoto Dreams. Look, I haven't given you your Miranda rights, so nothing you say can be held against you anyway, right? Talk to me."

Gray said nothing for a while. He lifted his chin. "If I tell you what I know, can you get me immunity for the fire? I never meant to hurt anyone."

"I can try."

His mouth downturned. "What good does that do me?"

"More good than if I don't try."

"Kick the gun away," he shouted. "Far away."

She did.

He came down the hill, taking care not to slip on the steep silty soil. Up close, he looked terrible. She could see that he'd hardly slept and had the sunken face of a man who hadn't eaten well and was near the end of his rope. He lowered his rifle slightly, his hand still near the trigger.

Rebecca tried her best to sound comforting. "You have nothing to fear from us. We're on your side. Why don't we go somewhere—into town, maybe—and talk about what happened."

"I'm not going anywhere," Connor said, his grip tightening as he lifted the rifle a bit higher.

"Okay. It's okay," Rebecca said. "Tell you what, why don't we all just sit down here, and you can fill us in on what happened." With that, she and Richie sat on the ground and waited.

Connor studied them a moment and then did the same. After a minute or so of silence, Connor began his story.

"I was given the magazine assignment by Liv Wong. I'd written for her before, and she liked my style. It was supposed to be just a humorous piece about six hot bachelors who had businesses in San Francisco. But as soon as I began to look into them, I learned that none of them were what they appeared to be."

"Why not?" Rebecca asked.

"They all had problems—either with money, or their love lives, or business partners, or they were simply unhappy despite an image of being all about fun and fame."

"In other words, we were all normal guys," Richie said, disgust etching the lines along the sides of his mouth.

Connor looked nervously at Richie. "I followed simple investigative reporting procedure. I talked to the people I saw hanging around the bachelors at their places of business and their homes."

"Spying on us," Richie said.

Connor sighed. "Sorry. Most of it was pretty dull stuff, to tell the truth. I didn't think I had anything special and was going to write an article just the way it was conceived—light, fun, maybe a little risqué—but I stumbled across something strange at Kyoto Dreams."

Rebecca nodded in encouragement for him to continue.

"I went to the restaurant several times," Connor said. "Some beautiful and nice waitresses worked there, and I met one who seemed to enjoy talking to me. I had one of those little rooms where I sat on the floor on a grass mat—tatami, I guess. A sliding door made from that white Japanese paper would be kept shut as I ate. After I met the talkative waitress, the next two times I went there, I asked for her by name. Maybe she felt sorry for me dining all alone, and I'd usually order the cheapest thing on the menu, but she'd come in, sit a little while with me and pour my sake, and we'd talk a bit. From her, I learned that Tanaka had a fiancée in Japan. I had already seen him with a number of different women. Some even came to the restaurant at closing time to wait for him.

They'd go out nightclubbing from there. He was definitely a party guy."

Richie folded his arms and scowled.

At the fierce look, Connor's hands tightened on the rifle stock. "Anyway, I discovered that Tanaka often left before closing time, and went out the back door. Since I was going broke eating at Kyoto Dreams, I decided to hang out in the alley and follow Tanaka from there. But I soon noticed some strange goings on. Like clockwork, a white van with no lettering on it would arrive at nine o'clock, and a small exchange would be made. It didn't look like food.

"After watching this three nights in a row, I followed the van. It went to a house in the Mission district—on Twenty-ninth Street. I soon switched from watching the restaurant to watching the house. It had plenty of goings and comings, but nobody lived there. It was some sort of drop-off location."

"For what?" Rebecca asked.

"I don't know. Drugs, most likely. That area is notorious for them."

Richie glanced at her and nodded. They had a good idea exactly which house Connor had stumbled across.

"As I watched the van," Connor continued, "I saw that it started its route around seven in the evening. One night, I followed it from the Mission district house. It wasn't easy, and a couple of times I lost it. But on the third try, I tracked it to the alley behind Easy Street Clothiers. Again, there was a strange exchange, but this time, a bunch of boxes were brought inside the store. It actually looked like it might be a legitimate delivery. The white van got there at seven-thirty; the store had closed at seven. Everyone seemed to have gone home but Diego Bosque.

"I watched Easy Street's back alley a few more nights. The van always showed up at precisely seven-thirty. Sometimes it would leave off boxes, other times, the only exchange was something small. And always, Diego Bosque would be the one to close up the store."

"Interesting," Rebecca murmured.

"I also knew Bosque was a frequent visitor to Kyoto Dreams," Connor said. "I would have liked to believe it was strictly for the food, but somehow, that didn't seem to be the case. I also tried to interview Kyoto Dreams employees about the receipt and shipment of goods late at night, but no one would talk to me. I knew something slippery was going on there, probably with some very dangerous people.

"By now, I'll admit that watching the van, the two businesses, and wanting to know what was going on, had become an obsession. I also saw, every day, soon after the restaurant opened, its manager would walk to a small business. Everything was written in Japanese, so I couldn't even tell what it was. One day, I said what the hell and walked in and asked if it was a Japanese travel agency. The one man in the office said no, that it was a bank. All I can tell you is it had damn few customers."

"Did you get its name?" Rebecca asked.

"No. I couldn't read anything, and the man's English wasn't the best. But I did some research and learned that the Yakuza, the 'Japanese mafia,' are involved with a number of such small 'personal' banks and other white collar institutions. I was pretty sure I'd just stumbled across one such business. I also learned the Yakuza are attempting to move many of their operations to places outside Japan. To do it, they formed front companies." Connor paused a moment, looking from Rebecca to Richie, and then said, "I believe both Kyoto Dreams and Easy Street Clothiers are two such companies."

"Damn," Richie muttered.

"Everything I saw told me this story is about a lot more than a male version of 'Sex in the City.' I was really excited about it, frankly, and decided to put hints in my article that something big is going on."

"Hold it, hold it," Richie interrupted. "You stumble across something that might be the Yakuza and you decide to jab at it? Are you friggin' crazy? Why not just go to the cops?"

"I wanted to build enough interest that people would want to know much more. Crime, sex, drugs—they sell," Connor said. "And I would be the guy with the information. I could turn it into a book, you know, True Crime. And once I had that, I could shop it to Hollywood."

"You *are* crazy," Richie said, his mouth wrinkled in disgust.

"But not crazy enough to investigate them directly. I hoped others would do it. But I also knew that a story in the *San Francisco Beat* would have no following unless something were done that would put it under the nose of every journalist in the city and beyond." He swallowed hard. "I decided a good way to get that attention would be to light a small fire at each place of business. Not a big fire, but just enough of one to get someone to put two and two together ... and come up with six, as in the six bachelors."

"You piece of shit!" Richie bellowed. "One of those places was mine!"

Rebecca gave him a quick glare. "Go on," she said to Connor.

Connor turned paler and shakier and tried not to look at Richie as he did as Rebecca asked.

"Of course, I wanted the attention to be with Kyoto Dreams and Easy Street. With things like this, it's the first few that get noticed. Others are just collateral damage."

"Collateral ...? I'm going to kill him, Rebecca," Richie muttered.

"The first fire I lit was the Easy Street Clothiers storeroom. It was easy to reach, and the store was popular with the right people. I didn't want to go to Kyoto Dreams next—that would be too obvious. So, I debated which place should be second. The hotel had all kinds of security because of their clientele, Logan Travis' home was a fortress, and although the tour boat company was usually locked up at night and easy pickings, it had scheduled a huge private party. When I learned Big Caesar's was closed on Monday night, it was no contest. I torched it."

Rebecca's hand clamped down hard on Richie's arm before he had a chance to react. He gave her such a hard look, she actually found it a bit unnerving.

"The next morning, I reached Kyoto Dreams a little after six," Connor continued. "I expected it to be completely empty, but as I was approaching the alley, a black car turned into it. I hurried towards the alley to see where the car was going, and why it was there so early. I hid where I could see into the alleyway, but I was pretty sure no one could see me. The black car stopped by the restaurant. A man got out, and put a black bag in the dumpster, then got back into the car and drove off."

"What kind of car?" Richie asked.

"I don't know. It was still dark at that time in the morning, and the car was black. It looked like a good-size sedan."

"So then what did you do?" Rebecca asked.

"As soon as the car left, I looked in the dumpster. I'd brought gloves for the arson and used them as I opened the bag. When I saw what was in it, I started to run out of the alley. But as I did, I saw a car at the entrance. I don't know if it was the same one or not. All I know is I ran in the opposite direction. The car turned into the alley and sped towards me. Near the corner, a small, neighborhood grocery had its back door propped open, probably airing the place out as it started business. I ran inside, through the store, and out the front door. I kept running down streets, through alleys. I also kept seeing dark cars turning in my direction. I have no idea if I was being paranoid—with good reason—or if someone was after me. All I know is, I was scared."

"With good reason, as you said," Rebecca told him.

Connor nodded. "I thought so. I also thought that it would be easy—if whoever tossed the head had connections to Kyoto Dreams—for them to find out who I was since I'd used credit cards to pay for my meals. It made me afraid to go home."

"You didn't think to report finding the head to the police?"

"The front page of the *Chronicle* told about a man dying in the Easy Street fire—and also mentioned the Big Caesar's fire, plus the connection to the *Beat* article. And I was responsible for the death of the man in the first fire. So now, not only was a murderer after me, but the police as well. I had no idea what to do. My plan for publicity was working—but it gave anyone who was looking for me my name.

"I took a room in a hotel, but it cost money and I had little. A couple of days of this went by, and then I decided to go to Richie. I had gotten hints from people who talked to him that he knew how to make things go away, to fix problems, and I definitely had a problem I needed fixed."

"You're such a dumbass." Richie scowled.

Connor lifted his rifle. "That's no way to talk to a man who's armed!"

"Maybe you'll shoot me and put me out of the misery of having to talk to a dickhead like you!"

"Please," Rebecca said to Connor. "Tell me what happened."

"Well, I'd once followed Richie from his club to his house." Connor spoke to Rebecca as if Richie wasn't even there. "So I went there. I saw the lights on, but I was worried about who might be there with him. I parked and decided to sneak around back to look in the window to see if Richie was alone. But for some reason, by the time I'd reached the yard, the lights had gone off. I almost left, but the more I thought about it, I decided to see what I could. I mean, maybe he shut them to watch TV? I crept up to the deck and to the kitchen window, only to find

Richie staring back at me. You two know what happened next." He looked at Richie. "You could probably use some motion detector lights in your yard."

"You son of a—"

"Not a bad idea," Rebecca said. "Given the kind of people who seem to come looking for you!"

Richie glared. "You're taking his side?"

"In this," she stated.

"Well, if you two are done arguing," Connor went on, "that was when I left the city. I remembered this abandoned shack from when I was a teenager and would come out this way to party. How did you find me?"

"None of your goddamned business!" Richie bellowed.

"You really need to come in with me," Rebecca said. "It's too dangerous for you here."

"It's a lot more dangerous for me to go into the city as long as a murderer is looking for me. I can't do it!"

"The best thing for you to do is to give us all the information you have. Work with us to catch the killer. It might help you with your other ... situation."

"I don't know," he said.

"She's right," Richie told him. "Now, don't shoot. I'm just getting out my wallet." Richie pulled out a couple of tens and held them out for Connor. "Get yourself a decent meal. I can't stand to see anyone, even an asshole, starving. After that, you might be able to think more clearly. If anyone can protect you, it's Inspector Mayfield."

Connor looked stunned that Richie would help him. Actually, so was Rebecca. She figured the hungrier he got, the more likely he'd be to turn himself in.

Still holding the rifle on them, Connor grabbed the money and backed away until he got back into the trees. There, he turned and ran.

"God, but I hate guns pointed at me." Richie faced Rebecca. They still sat on the ground. "If that SOB had decided to shoot first and talk later, I'm hoping you're wearing that little ankle pistol you often carry."

She hiked up her jeans leg just a little way, and the pistol was visible. The way she'd been sitting, it was in easy reach.

Richie grinned. "A badass, all right."

21

When they returned to San Francisco, Richie called Shay who had been working on the data Rebecca had sent him about Kyoto Dreams and Easy Street.

Richie gave Shay a quick rundown of Connor Gray's explanation.

"That confirms what I'm seeing," Shay said.

"Which is?" Richie asked.

"Both businesses were in financial trouble a couple of years back, and then, while teetering on the edge of bankruptcy, they both began making more money than ever before. Want to meet?"

They agreed to meet at a coffee shop near Shay's home in the Presidio Heights area.

Shay only had coffee, but Rebecca and Richie each ordered large, meaty sandwiches and fries, both feeling hungry after their foray into the north bay. Then Shay took over.

"It's money laundering," he said.

"So Courtney was right," Richie said. "Pierre told me what she'd said about money laundering through the LA Fashion District."

"I don't get it," Rebecca said. "I mean, can you really launder much money through a clothing shop?"

"Through a high-end one you can," Shay said. "Bosque's shop used a clothing manufacturer in China to send shipments of clothes they made at low cost to Easy Street. Their invoices, however, showed much pricier merchandise than it was. When the clothes sold, the books were rigged to show that they sold for more than they really did. All those extra funds were then deposited in cash into a bank account as a formal, legal transaction from the sale of the clothes."

"So that means," Rebecca said, "all the extra cash the store is depositing, must have come from the sale of drugs, right?"

"Exactly," Shay told her. "In this way, the cash deposits skirt the warning flags provided by current financial transparency laws and regulations, and so the drug money is washed."

"Any type of trade across international borders," Richie said, "is an opportunity for illegal transactions to be buried among the billions of legal ones. I'm not saying there's any connection between the growth of international trade deals and drugs entering the country, or with rich people and politicians becoming wealthier than ever, but it might be more than a coincidence."

"Soon after this started," Shay added, "Bosque opened three more stores. It looks like he probably laundered around three thousand a day in San Francisco alone, so who knows how much money, in total, was involved."

"And the same sort of thing was done with Kyoto Dreams?" Rebecca asked. "But restaurants don't do nearly the business of a clothing store, I would think."

"Restaurants are commonly used for laundering," Richie said. "Did you ever watch the TV show, *Breaking Bad*? A restaurant called Los Pollos Hermanos was a front for all kinds of things."

"The strange thing about restaurants," Shay said, "is the best ones for money laundering are those with the least customers. Let's say a restaurant has no customers. On its books, it shows all fake information—maybe that it bought $1000 worth of food, paid $1000 for staff, rent, etc., and sold $3000 worth of food in a day. They deposit $3000 as profit from the restaurant, but in fact, it's all cash from drug money. They keep showing this pattern, every day, on their books—varying the amounts a bit, of course. But every day they withdraw some money from the bank and make a deposit of cash from drug deals. In my example, in a week, if the restaurant is open every day, they can launder $21,000 in drug money and not serve one customer. The problem comes in when the restaurant starts to attract real customers. When that happens, it has to actually buy some food, hire cooks and waiters, and so on. The more customers, the less room for fraud since restaurants, depending on size and what they serve, do have a finite amount of money they can make without attracting government or bank regulator notice."

"Did they make the deposits into the small Japanese bank that Connor Gray talked about?"

Shay shook his head. "I doubt it. The one used here is a mid-sized, legitimate bank."

Rebecca thought about all she'd learned. "So what happened? With all this planning and so on, why were Tanaka and Bosque killed?"

"Who knows?" Shay said. "Maybe something scared them and they wanted to get out of the business. Ironically, Bosque's businesses might actually have done well on their own. He had gotten a good reputation for style, even if not the quality of the clothes he sold. And, it might be he didn't like hearing about the low quality. He started invoicing a lot of wholesale clothes from the US, UK, and Italy, and I suspect those were legitimate. Kyoto

Dreams books, on the other hand, looked like Tanaka might have continued to struggle."

"Shay is saying," Richie interrupted, "that what was going on in these men's lives that caused them to become targets isn't showing up in the numbers he's looking at. That's up to us to figure out."

"It makes sense," Rebecca said. "But it also means there were more people involved than just Bosque and Tanaka. They needed others to work on the books for them, make bank deposits and withdrawals, and so on."

"And that kind of coordination can lead to problems. Or jealousy. Or who knows what," Shay said.

"It seems, Rebecca," Richie said, "someone needs to look into who's tampering with the invoices and books at Easy Street and Kyoto Dreams. That'll tell you who's doing the money laundering, although it still doesn't pinpoint your murderer."

"True, but it gets us closer, I'm sure," Rebecca said. "Shay, thank you!"

"Remember," Richie said, "Shig Tanaka was a friend. He might have crossed a line because he felt desperate, but nobody deserved to be killed the way he was. I want to know who killed him and see that justice is done."

Rebecca shuddered at his words. "We'll figure it out. I promise."

22

———————

As Rebecca stepped onto the elevator the next morning for the ride up to the homicide bureau, instead of the usual excitement she felt going to her job, she was feeling almost defeated. The murders she was dealing with were ugly and sad, and despite all the criminal activity going on, there was no clear motive for the deaths, and therefore no clear suspect.

She filled Bill Sutter and Lt. Eastwood in on all she'd learned, claiming her source was a "confidential informant" who would remain confidential. Eastwood didn't press it. He decided they needed to let the Marin County sheriff's department know where Connor Gray was hiding and try to pick him up. Rebecca had a contact in the department there, Deputy Sheriff Mike Vargas. He was another good man that she might have been interested in dating were it not for Richie. Was she seeing a pattern here? In any case, she phoned Vargas and explained Connor Gray's role in her case, and where he was hiding out. She warned him of the potential danger involved in trying to arrest a nervous, paranoid man with a long-range rifle. Vargas assured her they'd be careful, and could handle it.

Then she drove to Kyoto Dreams before it opened and

waited outside in her SUV. Despite Tanaka's death, the restaurant continued to function. Only after Shay's money-laundering explanation did she understand why. It wasn't about the food.

Connor Gray had told her that the restaurant's manager, Kazue Hanemoto, would walk to a small Japanese bank branch office each day shortly after the restaurant opened. She sat, waiting to see if Connor was right.

Sure enough, Hanemoto soon appeared. She got out of the SUV and followed him two blocks to a small storefront. She took a photo of the Japanese characters showing its name and sent the photo to the interpreter she'd once used. The business appeared every bit as quiet and seemingly innocuous as Connor had described.

She soon received an answer. The name of the bank was "Asahi Ginko" which translated to "Morning Sun Bank." But, the interpreter pointed out, Asahi was also the name of a popular beer.

Back at her desk, she contacted the detective in Kyoto who had helped her when she first learned of Shig Tanaka's death. When she told him a little of what was going on and gave him the name of the bank Hanemoto entered, he sounded nervous. "Please, do not look into it any further. It is not a real bank. The people involved kill first, and they are protected. It is not anything for local police to try to handle."

With the Kyoto detective's warning ringing in her ears, she put in a call to Brandon Seymour, an FBI agent she had worked with in the past.

Seymour said he wasn't far from the Hall of Justice and not a half hour later, he reached her desk. He looked so much like a stereotype of an FBI agent—big, beefy, short blond hair, clear blue eyes, and wearing a dark suit, white shirt, and blue tie—it made her smile. Seeing his return smile, she realized she'd made a mistake. He had seemed a bit sweet on her from time to time. He tried not to show it, of course, but she suspected that if given the slightest encouragement, he would have.

"Good to see you again, Rebecca," he said.

She told him all she had found out about the possible money-laundering schemes going on in the city.

Seymour pursed his lips. "So now, Amalfi has you involved with international gangs. He's a real gem, isn't he?"

"No, a murder got me involved. It's my job."

"As I see it," Seymour sniffed, "the victim of that first fire has been all but forgotten."

Rebecca bristled. "And as I see it, I'm dealing with three murders. I assure you, I *never* forgot the first victim. The poor guy was in the wrong place at the wrong time, but his killing has been solved—Connor Gray confessed. He had a name, by the way—Benjamin Larkin. His death and the arson that caused it were catalysts for a whole series of crimes. And while I'm quite close to solving the murders of Tanaka and Bosque, I find their murders overlap into your jurisdiction. But if you aren't interested …"

"Calm down, Rebecca. I'm interested. Very much so. If the Yakuza is trying to move into this city, I want to know all about it."

"What I've got," she said, "is based on assumptions at this point, but good assumptions. If they're correct, I know you'll want to step in. We have quite enough problems with our home-grown gangs without leaving the door open for new ones."

Seymour went quiet as he looked over the data she gave him. "It looks to me as if you've got some deep sources. Do you think the person who gave you this would be willing to make contact with these people and nail down exactly who is doing what?"

"I doubt it."

"Right now," Seymour said, "if I were a betting man, I'd say Hanemoto is working with the Yakuza, and they decided he had to get rid of Tanaka. But I'd hate to have us tip our hand before we know exactly what's involved here."

"But the Thirteens and El Grande ..."

"They're fighting with Yakuza, that's clear enough."

"It may be a little more complicated," Rebecca murmured.

"Well, well, look who's here," Richie said as he strolled towards Rebecca's desk. He then gazed at Rebecca and she couldn't help but warmly smile—a smile that, she was sure, wasn't lost on Seymour.

"Amalfi," Seymour said with a frown. "I should have known." He faced Rebecca. "This is where you're getting your information, right?"

"A lot of it. We're friends, so why shouldn't he help me?"

Both Richie and Seymour looked at her with disbelief. Seymour sneered. "Friends?"

"That's what I said. And Richie's not involved. He was a victim."

"Oh, yes, that's right." Seymour hooked his arm over the back of the guest chair and looked up at Richie. "Somebody's supposed to be trying to kill you, right, Amalfi?"

Richie turned the full force of his glare on Seymour. "Whoever it is hasn't succeeded, as you can see."

"There's always hope."

"Funny man, Seymour. Maybe you want a job as a comedian at my club."

"I wouldn't stoop so low."

"Not to worry. You'd never get the job anyway."

"Will you boys stop it?" Rebecca said, giving them both a harsh glare until they calmed down. "I'd like to get back to business. Richie, I was just telling Brandon what we've found out about a potential Yakuza situation, and he was asking if we know anyone who could infiltrate the Kyoto Dreams group and find out exactly what's going on."

"Tell me a little more what you're thinking," Richie said to Seymour. "If you're thinking, that is."

"Richie!" Rebecca warned.

He held both hands up in a mock "I give up" type gesture.

Seymour gritted his teeth until the urge to snap back passed. "Okay, it's simple enough."

"It sure as hell couldn't be complicated," Richie muttered softly to Rebecca.

She rolled her eyes.

"As I was saying," Seymour said gruffly. "Someone needs to go in there. Maybe someone who can say he'd like to take over where Tanaka left off and see who takes the bait. Then we'll know who was working with Tanaka, and maybe even learn who killed him and why."

"From what little I've seen of the situation in Kyoto Dreams," Rebecca said, "they wouldn't trust anyone who just showed up and asked to become part of it. Shig Tanaka and his manager, Hanemoto, went to school together. I suspect most people involved have similar long-standing relationships, probably going back to when they were in Japan together. I don't see anyone winning over their confidence."

"She's absolutely right," Richie said.

Seymour grimaced.

"But there's another way," Richie said. "It's easy."

Both looked at him and waited.

"We don't go in there asking to be let in like some little wuss seeking a favor. Not like, oh, I don't know, Brandon Seymour might do. Instead, we go in and *tell* them what's up."

Seymour's face turned livid at the insult. "What the hell are you talking about, Amalfi? Nobody tells the Yakuza 'what's up.'"

Richie folded his arms. "I suspect the Yakuza aren't sitting around in Kyoto Dreams making fancy sushi dishes or bussing tables. The people I would talk to are Hanemoto and his staff."

"You?" Rebecca gasped.

"That's right. I'd go in there and tell them Shig was a friend of mine—which they know is true—and that I know all about what he was doing. Also true. Now that he's gone, I'm moving in. Either they take it, or I make my own deals with the money men, and they'll be cut out altogether."

Seymour looked disgusted. "Why in hell would they take a deal like that?"

"Because they're scared," Richie said. "I think whatever happened—and I've got an idea, but I'm not positive as yet—the people in the restaurant involved in the scheme are scared to death of two things. The first is losing the connection that's bringing in a lot of extra money for them, and the second is ending up like Shig. I don't know if they've decided which is the lesser of the two evils."

"You expect to be able to pull off something like that?" Seymour asked.

"Sure."

"No, you can't," Rebecca said. "You make it sound easy, but I can think of a million ways it can go very, very bad. To start, Hanemoto could decide there's no way he'd let you take over anything. If he's already killed his best friend, he'll have no qualms about pulling out a gun and shooting you on the spot."

"I'm sure my friends in the FBI won't let that happen," Richie said, facing Seymour. "Maybe I need to wear a wire so if anything goes wrong, you'll come rushing in like the cavalry, right Seymour?"

Seymour snorted.

"You can't do it, Richie," Rebecca insisted. "That group is too dangerous."

"Shig was my friend, and someone killed him. And I can't forget that my idea was the catalyst that ultimately got him killed. Who knows who they'll go after next."

"But this is simply too dangerous," she said.

"It's also the best and fastest way for it to end."

Rebecca vehemently shook her head. "You're a civilian. You can't—"

"Rebecca, I can," Richie said. He faced Seymour. "How do we do this?"

23

———

Richie sat in his car in the Hall of Justice parking lot and phoned Shay. He was definitely going to need his friend to help him make it out of this situation in one piece. He trusted the FBI, but not with his life. Plus, as he, Seymour, and Rebecca talked, an idea had formed—a dangerous idea, but well worth trying—and he needed Shay to pull it off.

They met at a coffee shop to work out the plan as much as possible, and then the two of them went to dinner at Kyoto Dreams. Richie had been stunned to learn it remained open after Shig Tanaka's death. That in itself was a huge red flag for what was going on.

As a waitress brought them to a tatami room, Richie gave her his card. "Please give this to Mr. Hanemoto. We would like to talk to him. It has to do with Mr. Tanaka."

Her eyes widened, and she hurried away. Another waitress brought them a bottle of warm sake and two small cups. She filled a cup for each of them and then left. They had no sooner finished the first cup than they were told Mr. Hanemoto would see them.

The two followed the waitress down a hall, past the

restrooms and kitchen. Two offices and a storeroom were located there. She knocked lightly and then opened the door to the first office. "Here is Mr. Hanemoto," she said to Richie and Shay bowing slightly, and then she left them.

A short, slight man with squared shoulders and a stiff demeanor stood as the two entered the room. He gave a small bow. "I am Hanemoto. I recognize you as one of Mr. Tanaka's friends"—he inclined his head towards Richie—"but not your companion." He faced Shay.

"This is Henry Tate, my associate. Henry, Mr. Hanemoto." It always struck Richie oddly using Shay's real name—Henry Ian Tate, III. He'd never learned where the nickname "Shay" came from, and knowing the guy, probably never would.

Hanemoto and Shay shook hands.

"You know," Shay said looking at both of them, "since this doesn't involve me, maybe I should just go back to the restaurant. I'd hate for the sake to get cold."

Richie nodded his agreement.

"It was a pleasure to meet you," Hanemoto said with a quick, stiff bow.

As soon as Shay left, Richie faced Hanemoto. "I'd like to set up a meeting. It should be sometime and someplace where we can talk at length, and openly, about the future."

Hanemoto's eyebrows rose with surprise. "I cannot imagine why you would request such a thing."

"Can't you?" Richie asked. Then, although he hadn't been invited to sit, he took a seat to show he wasn't going anywhere until a time and place was set for the requested meeting.

Later that night, Richie phoned Rebecca to say Hanemoto had

agreed to meet at Kyoto Dreams, but only at a time when no one else would be anywhere near: four o'clock in the morning.

Rebecca needed to relay the information to Seymour and work out the logistics to make sure Richie stayed safe. She also told Richie that although the FBI was in charge, she had gotten Lieutenant Eastwood to agree to have the San Francisco SWAT team on the scene and ready for a take-down, if it came to that. Although the FBI had various tactical squads, she personally knew many local SWAT members and trusted them. Still, the entire situation was making her quite nervous.

Richie told her he was at Big Caesar's, and would be there that night until closing time. She didn't need to ask why. He recognized the danger he would be walking into, and she suspected he was making some last minute plans "just in case." The thought made her stomach clench.

Alone in her apartment, she tried to nap, but her mind was so filled with all that could go wrong with Seymour and Richie's plan that sleep wouldn't come. Richie wasn't trained in under-cover operations and hadn't signed up for this kind of danger.

At two fifteen in the morning, he arrived.

She opened the door and put her arms around him. "It's not too late to change your mind."

He held her close a long moment. "If I did, I'd have to spend a lot of my time looking over my shoulder. We've got to get rid of these people."

"It doesn't have to be your fight," she said.

"Doesn't it? Too many fingers have pointed at me, including El Effin' Grande and maybe the Yakuza." He walked to the sofa and sat, leaning forward. "Worse, I've got an idea about what might have really happened, and if I'm right, tonight will end what might grow and fester into a blood bath. So, since I'm already caught up in it, I'm in the best position to stop it."

"But you shouldn't be." She sat beside him, her hand on his back.

"I know what these people are like," he said, "and what they're capable of if they get unhappy. It ain't pretty."

"I wish it didn't have to be you," she whispered.

"Hell, you aren't the only one!" he admitted.

She tried to smile, but couldn't quite manage it. His phone buzzed. It was a text message. He read it, and his mouth tightened. Who, she wondered, was sending a message at two-thirty in the morning? "What's happening?"

"Nothing unexpected," he said as he put the phone back in his pocket. He faced her. "Let's think about something else for a while. Tell me, was your sister another one who suggested you stay away from me?"

She warmed at the memory. "Not hardly. She liked you, and when you tried to rescue her from those goons, wow!" Her gaze became intense. "She also said something odd, that we need to stop listening to what we *say* to each other, and listen more to what she suspects runs deeper."

He looked a bit perplexed, but slowly his expression eased to a gentle smile. "I think I like your sister," he murmured. He put his arm around her and they held each other close as the last few minutes ticked by before it was time to meet Seymour.

24

At three in the morning, Rebecca and Richie drove to the FBI parking lot in the Federal building. Seymour met them and led them to a van filled with the government's listening equipment and monitoring system. A technician put a wire on Richie under his shirt and then checked to be sure it was working properly. Feeling the wire against his skin made everything he'd agreed to do that much more real—and deadly.

Rebecca said nothing, but the look in her eyes said it all. He knew she was worried about this, and that didn't make him feel any better about it. The hardest part was the waiting, sitting in that little, claustrophobic van with Rebecca, Seymour, and a couple of others, watching the hands of the clock slowly tick by.

Finally, it was seven minutes before four. In the empty, early morning streets, the parking lot was only a few minutes away from Kyoto Dreams. Time to go. Rebecca looked scarcely able to move, and he gave her hand a quick squeeze as he stepped out of the van. With the FBI and SWAT teams in place, Richie got into his Porsche.

But before he started down this road, he had one last thing he needed to do.

He took out his phone and deleted the liar app. He had rarely seen an employee work as hard as Tommy Ginnetti in getting Big Caesar's up and running again, and he believed Rebecca sometimes even more than he believed himself. He didn't need any stinkin' app trying to cast doubts on them. As the deletion protocol ended, he was glad to have the sleazy thing out of his life.

That done, he started the Porsche. On Polk Street, he drove a few blocks north until he needed to turn off to reach the alley behind Kyoto Dreams. There, he stopped at the back door of the restaurant. The sound of the Porsche helped mask any footsteps that might have been heard as a few members of the SWAT team moved closer. They had all agreed the most natural thing was for Richie to drive as close as possible to the meeting point.

He got out of his Porsche, lightly ran a hand over the back of his hair to smooth it, and tugged at the cuffs of his white shirt so they formed a sharp line against his suit jacket. He then walked to the back door and knocked. A Japanese man he'd never seen before cracked it open. The man said nothing, but nodded and opened the door wider. Richie entered. The man locked the door behind him and then led him to Hanemoto's office.

Rebecca stayed in the van and rode with Seymour closer to the restaurant. The driver parked on Van Ness Avenue, a busy street, a block and a half from Kyoto Dreams. "Aren't you too far away?" she asked.

"We can hear from this point," Seymour said. "If we get any closer, we risk being noticed. I'm sure they have people watching the street—just as we do."

She couldn't see a thing from where they were parked; it was maddening. "Is the SWAT team close enough?"

"They're your people, not ours. I think my guys could have handled it just fine, but your boss can be a real ass when he wants to."

"But you are coordinating with them, right?," she asked.

"Yes, Rebecca. You can stop worrying. Your boyfriend will be fine."

"He's not ..." she began, then stopped. Who was she kidding?

She rubbed her fingers nervously. It was all well and good for Seymour to tell her everything would be fine, but how the hell did he know?

Hanemoto was seated at his desk and stood as Richie approached. The two shook hands and then Hanemoto poured them each a single malt Scotch. He handed a glass to Richie. "*Kampai.*"

Richie repeated the toast. Both took a sip and then moved to a round table and sat.

"I know you were Tanaka-san's friend," Hanemoto said, "so I will listen. But I believe this meeting may be a waste of both our times."

"I know what's been going on here," Richie told him. "I know about your fake accounting books, and about your money laundering. I want in. That's all. I intend to become a part of it."

Hanemoto's expression flitted between mirth and outrage. "Ridiculous! I don't know what you're talking about."

"It's way past time for games," Richie said. "You aren't good enough or important enough to handle this on your own. You need me. Tanaka is dead, and many people think you killed him."

A look of disgust came over Hanemoto's face. "If so, they are stupid." Hanemoto sneered. "He was my friend. I would never do such a thing."

Richie nodded. He believed Hanemoto, and understood the man's outrage. He took a different tactic. "Tanaka told me he was getting tired of what was going on here. The restaurant was doing well, but he was in too deep to take his profits and leave."

"You don't know that."

Richie shrugged. "Don't I? People talk to me. It's what I do. That's why my business is perfect for the kind of thing you're doing. Right now, I work much harder for my money than you've had to, and I'm tired of it. You're getting a nice cut just for keeping a phony set of books. It's a great business. And my nightclub can hide a whole lot more money than a restaurant. Working with me, your rewards will be much greater than they've ever been here."

Hanemoto's eyebrows twitched at the word "your." "But, therefore, the danger will be even higher."

"Without Tanaka, you don't have a restaurant." Richie's words, his tone, were harsh and firm. "You've tried to keep it running, but it's just a matter of time before there are more questions than you have answers—like why you're charging top chef prices when you have little more than a short-order cook in your kitchen. You have to know that."

"My chef can learn," Hanemoto said defiantly. "Or we will find another."

"And raise a lot of suspicion. Kyoto Dreams' location is prominent and expensive; its reputation was high with Tanaka, as were its prices. To stay open now that he's gone will create a lot of curiosity. Curiosity that you can't afford."

As the argument continued, Hanemoto looked defeated and older than his years. "Kyoto Dreams was Tanaka's personal dream," he said. "I hate to see it die the way he did."

"You have no choice," Richie insisted. "I think it's time you consider changing the structure of this business. Close Kyoto Dreams and use your business skills elsewhere. Perhaps with me," Richie said.

"Why should I trust you?" Hanemoto asked.

Richie paused before answering. "Let's turn that question around," he said finally. "Many people think you killed Tanaka, your friend. If they think you're that kind of man, with that sort of character, perhaps I'm the one who should be suspicious. Why should I trust you?"

"I said I did not kill him!" Hanemoto all but growled the words.

Richie eyed the man, then, with his voice barely above a whisper, said, "I believe you. I never thought you would kill him. But what I don't understand is why he had to die."

Hanemoto finished his Scotch. Now, it was his turn to reflect before speaking. "There is a saying in Japan that goes something like, 'if you do not enter the tiger's cave, you will not catch its cub.' Tanaka entered the tiger's cave many years ago. Perhaps his death was inevitable."

"What do you mean?" Richie asked.

"Tanaka-san worked with the Yakuza in Kyoto. They helped him get started when he needed them, so he was loyal to them. He also thought, once he left Japan, that phase of his life would be over, and that he was free of them. But then, here in San Francisco, they came to call. They are trying to spread beyond Japan, you see."

Richie nodded.

"They came at a time when the restaurant was struggling, when there were economic troubles both here and in Japan. Tanaka thought he might need to close all his restaurants, declare bankruptcy. They offered a way to keep them open. He went along, but even so, he hated having them, again, in his business.

And then, El Grande and his men discovered that the Yakuza were attempting to move into El Grande's territory. The two battled, and apparently, the Yakuza was not yet strong enough in San Francisco to fight them off. El Grande demanded we continue the money laundering scheme, but that we work for him now. And then, because of Tanaka's former ties with the Yakuza, and because of their threats against his family and fiancée in Japan, he couldn't get away from them completely. We laundered money for El Grande, but half of our profits from that went to the Yakuza."

Rebecca couldn't handle sitting in the cramped van and listening to Richie and Hanemoto talk.

If the Yakuza had no part in any of this, and Richie was in no danger, everything would be fine and it didn't matter what he and Hanemoto were talking about.

But if Richie was in danger, and if Yakuza killers were lurking around him, what good would it do for her to be in a van a block and a half away?

"I'm moving closer," she said.

"Relax," Seymour ordered.

She tried, but couldn't. Every nerve in her body screamed that something was wrong. This was going too quietly, too peacefully. She didn't trust it.

She got out of the van and pulled the hood of her black sweatshirt up to cover her blond hair, then crept along the buildings towards Polk Street. She knew most of the SWAT team had been stationed in the alley at the back of the restaurant. She expected far fewer men were covering the front.

She headed that way, moving slowly and staying in the shadows.

~

"So you were being squeezed," Richie said. "El Grande pushed the Yakuza out of his territory—at least temporarily—but they kept their claws in you because of Tanaka's fears for his family. Tell me, did you keep a separate set of books or what?"

"We didn't dare. If El Grande found out, he may have wanted an even larger cut than he was taking. I kept everything in my head. Our transactions with the Yakuza were all in cash as much as possible. I handled it personally." Hanemoto folded his hands and paused a while before continuing. "In the end, Tanaka wanted to get away from both of them—the Yakuza as well as El Grande. When he was talking to you and Pierre Fontaine at lunch that day, and all of you thought about a way to get some free publicity, he jumped at the chance. You see, his reputation as a top chef was growing. Major restaurants wanted him, which would have meant much more money and less work for him. But he needed a way to get out of the shackles around him here. And then, he thought he found a way."

"How?"

"Last Monday, there was a fire at Diego Bosque's shop in the morning and at your club in the evening. Diego and Tanaka met that night—apparently they went out drinking. They were convinced the arsons had something to do with the *San Francisco Beat* article, but they didn't know what. Late that same night, very late, in fact, Tanaka called me. He was very drunk, probably high as well, but very excited to tell me his plan. He said it came to him while he was with Bosque. The two had argued, in fact. Bosque thought the idea was dangerous, foolish, even. But he insisted Bosque was wrong. He was going to do whatever it took. That was the last I heard from him."

~

The perpetual San Francisco fog had rolled in off the ocean through the Golden Gate, covering the moon and stars, and blanketing the street lamps in a foggy haze. No lights shown through windows and only an occasional set of car headlights going by illuminated the area as Rebecca crept toward Polk Street. Once she reached it, she didn't see any SWAT team members. She could only assume they must be near and well-hidden.

A car drove by, and she ducked into the doorway of a storefront.

She wasn't sure if it was a good thing or not that Richie had been inside the restaurant for what seemed like an eternity. She would have hoped that by now, he'd have the information he'd gone inside for, and would safely walk out having captured everything on tape. If so, the SWAT team would move in and arrest Hanemoto.

But none of that was happening.

She noticed a movement up ahead, much closer to the restaurant than where she was currently. She froze and watched, but whoever was there, was too far from her to see in the dark. She hoped it was a SWAT team member.

But soon, another car drove by, illuminating the man before he stepped into the doorway to hide himself. He wasn't dressed in the SWAT helmet or body armor.

This was all wrong. Seymour was too far away to offer any help. If whoever was there was up to no good, Rebecca would have to stop him herself, especially since there was no way to warn Richie.

"What was Tanaka's plan?" Richie asked.

Hanemoto sucked his breath between his teeth and thought

a moment before answering. "He believed the arsonist would strike Kyoto Dreams soon. And he was glad. Very glad. In fact, if the arsonist didn't go after it, Tanaka might have. He was sick of this life and planned to go to London for a fresh start. But instead, he was killed. And the way his body was found told everyone that if they ever even *thought* about walking away from El Grande, let alone tried to do it, they would get the same treatment."

Richie swallowed hard. He'd been right in what he'd suspected had happened to Tanaka, but it was still difficult to hear. "You're saying that Tanaka spoke to Diego Bosque and then was killed?"

"Yes. Bosque was a part of El Grande's inner circle. I had suspected as much, and even heard rumors that the two were related through El Grande's marriage, but Tanaka refused to believe any of that. He thought Bosque was simply a good man who had gotten into trouble and was being squeezed in the same way as he was. Obviously, Bosque told El Grande what Tanaka planned, and that resulted in Tanaka being killed."

Richie nodded. "I see. And now"—his eyes were hard as he looked at Hanemoto—"I know who killed Diego Bosque."

Hanemoto's nostrils flared. "I was glad to take his life. His betrayal killed my friend. Tanaka-san and I were like brothers. I had to avenge him. You understand."

Richie understood completely.

From the doorway behind him, Richie heard a slightly accented voice, one he recognized well after being captured and questioned by the man. "That's all I wanted to know."

Rebecca crept from doorway to doorway, inching closer to the mysterious man watching the restaurant. His back was to her. As she darted for the next doorway, he stepped away from the wall and the alcove where he'd hidden. She froze, pushing herself back flat against the wall. He appeared to be holding a monster .50 caliber cannon, while his head swiveled from side to side as if perusing the surrounding area. Her heart pounded. Had he heard her footsteps?

Rebecca hoped the night and the fog would keep her safe.

She saw a car turn onto Polk, and prayed the gunman wasn't looking in her direction as the car drove by, knowing it would illuminate her just as it did the rest of the street.

As the car neared, she watched the stranger, ready to act if he spotted her. Instead, the car lights drove him back a little way into his hidey-hole. But as it neared him, she was now close enough to see the outline of a skinny body, and a scraggly mustache and long goatee.

She gasped. He was the same man as she'd seen in the room with El Grande when holding Richie prisoner.

Hanemoto's bodyguard scarcely had time to react before El Grande's gunman fired a bullet into his heart.

Hanemoto reached for his pistol, but too late. All of El Grande's attention had been focused on him, as if wanting to be sure the manager knew exactly what was going to happen to him, and who was going to do it. El Grande himself pointed his gun and fired, killing Hanemoto with one shot to the middle of his forehead.

At the sound of gunfire from inside the restaurant, Rebecca turned her head towards it, dread and anguish filling her. That was when she first saw members of the SWAT team. They had moved a couple of steps closer to the restaurant, but held there as if awaiting orders. What was wrong with them? She couldn't believe what she was seeing.

Why aren't they moving in?

~

Richie jumped to his feet as El Grande sauntered deeper into the room, sneering at its small size and cheap furnishing. With him was the manager of Easy Street, Dan Peters, and a gunman. Peters had a gas canister and started dousing all the furniture with it, along with the bodies of Hanemoto and his guard.

"Richie, my friend," El Grande said, his voice soft and sad. "I'm sorry. But even though you found out that Hanemoto killed Diego—and I appreciate being allowed to avenge my family's honor—I'm going to have to kill you. It's not personal, but I don't like witnesses."

"El Grande, you don't have to do this," Richie said, a hand outstretched as he backed towards the wall.

The click of a lighter was heard and then a rush as a fire began.

The sound was followed by four gunshots in rapid succession.

And then all went quiet.

~

Rebecca felt as if her heart would stop as four more gunshots sounded in the quiet of the night. She saw in her peripheral vision that the SWAT team was finally moving. They ran along the opposite side of the street towards the restaurant. But she forced herself to remain still, to focus all her attention on the skinny mustached man. He took a half-step forward, and with his massive semi-automatic, aimed directly at the SWAT team.

"Police! Drop the gun," Rebecca yelled, her Glock pointed at El Grande's man. "Or this time, I *will* kill you."

The man's arm whipped in her direction. He fired at the same time as she pulled the trigger.

25

———————

Rebecca stood still, stunned and horrified by all that had just happened.

El Grande's man lay on the sidewalk, dead. His bullet missed by an inch or less, but her shot had been true.

She dropped her gun and looked up. She didn't know how long she had stood there, but now she saw that the SWAT team had knocked open the front doors of the restaurant. Smoke was billowing out of it, a lot of smoke. She had no idea why. No idea what had happened inside, except for the barrage of gunshots she'd heard.

She took a step towards it when Lt. Eastwood, who had decided to show up for the joint FBI-SFPD action, grabbed her wrist and clamped down hard. "Let the SWAT team take it," he commanded. "Stay out of their way!"

She nodded, and Eastwood let her go, telling her the SWAT team had been ordered in as soon as El Grande started to talk, and the first gunshots were heard. They had hit the back door, the one off the alley, with a battering ram. The door sprang open, but as soon as the outside air hit the flames, they roared large and deadly, and the SWAT team had been forced to back up.

He explained that the go-ahead was then given to the few members at the front of the restaurant to breach the scene. A couple of them had seen the shoot-out she was involved in. They saw the gunman aim at them, and even before they reacted, they watched Rebecca stop him. They saw the exchange of fire before she managed to take him down. She'd had what Eastwood called "a good shoot."

Rebecca shut her eyes, suddenly light-headed. It may have been a good shoot here, but she'd also heard the gunshots from inside the restaurant. They still resounded over and over in her head. Two shots, a brief pause, and then four more. No one could survive that.

She felt an arm around her shoulders, holding her, supporting her. "You okay, partner?" To her surprise, it was Sutter.

She couldn't answer.

He bowed his head and soon let her go.

She stepped a bit closer to the building's front entrance, even as she dreaded what she would find. But the SWAT had established a perimeter, and she wasn't allowed past it. She could see that the front door had been opened, and thick smoke poured out of it, but no flames were visible.

The outline of a man appeared in the smoke-filled doorway. A SWAT member tried to help him, but he waved him off as he staggered away from the building.

Even with a handkerchief over his mouth, bent and stumbling, she recognized him. She knew she always would.

Rebecca moved towards him.

"Wait!" Lieutenant Eastwood said.

But she didn't listen. She pushed past perimeter and ran to Richie, who was coughing so much he could barely walk. "I've got him," she said to the SWAT officer still trying to help, then did a double-take. Even with a helmet on, she'd recognize those blue eyes anywhere—it was Shay. She gawked as he gave a quick nod and then rushed off in the opposite direction. Her arm circled Richie's waist, and he leaned against her for support.

She helped him to a spot where the air was clear. He had stopped coughing and was able to stand without support. His face and clothes were black with soot, and his eyes watered, but to her, he looked wonderful.

"Are you hurt?" she asked, brushing his hair back from his eyes, touching his face, his shoulders, his arms as if to convince herself he was still alive.

"I'll be okay."

"You scared me half to death, you know!"

"I didn't mean to."

"No, I guess not." She put her arms around him.

He hesitated to hold her. "Everyone's watching," he whispered.

She caught his eyes. "Let them." Then, in front of Lt. Eastwood, the other detectives, the FBI, God, and everyone else who might be near, she kissed him and hugged him as if she never wanted to let him go.

26

———

Much to Rebecca's surprise, Lt. Eastwood told her to go home. El Grande, his gunman, Dan Peters, Hanemoto, and his bodyguard had all died. The crime scene had been secured and would be processed. The next day, she'd have some paperwork to fill out because of the shooting she'd been involved in, but already the man she'd killed had been identified as a murderer of at least ten people—but no one had dared to testify against him. She was sorry to take any life, but at least she'd stopped him from adding to his total.

Richie was being questioned by Seymour in his van and she had not been invited to listen in. Seymour kept a strict dividing line between "his" FBI areas, and SFPD areas of responsibility. She didn't care. She knew Richie would fill her in on the details.

She waited for him.

When he stepped out of the van, he looked both emotionally and physically exhausted. He stared at her a moment without a hint of a smile and then shook his head.

"I'm taking you home," she said.

"I heard what happened," he told her, his expression harsh and intense as he studied her. "Are you all right?"

"Yes. Quite."

"I mean, not just physically, but—"

"Yes. I can handle it. Really."

He put his arms around her, and held her close, showing his support for her just as she had earlier for him. Her sister's words, that if she'd been shot Richie would be there for her, came back to her, and her arms tightened around him.

Then he let her go, his eyes sad but also with admiration. He handed over the keys to his beloved Porsche without even making a quip about it.

"You're actually going to let me drive?" she said.

"Just don't strip the gears," he murmured.

"Gears? What are those?" she teased.

He put his arm across her shoulders, she put hers across his back, and he let her lead him to the car.

He fell asleep as she drove and didn't wake up until she shut off the engine inside his garage.

In the kitchen, he spoke drowsily, "I don't know what you want to eat or drink at this ungodly hour, but help yourself. I've got to take a shower to get the stink of this night off me."

"Maybe I should call a cab—"

"No." His expression told her how much he was hurting and didn't want to be alone. "Stay. I'll just be a minute."

She nodded.

She looked in the refrigerator. She didn't want to eat, and she was pretty sure food was the last thing he wanted.

She found a bottle of cabernet sauvignon that had been opened, and poured them each a glass, then went into the living room. She switched on his gas fireplace to take the chill out of the air. Nights in San Francisco usually had a damp chill that cut right through you, and that night, she realized now that she actually had time to think about the weather, had been no different.

He soon came into the living room wearing black sweatpants and a blue sweatshirt. His hair was still damp, but the soot and smoky smell were gone. He sat beside her on the sofa and picked up the wine glass. "To a job completed," he said. *"Salut'."*

She lifted her glass. *"Salut',"* she said in return as their glasses clinked.

He took a small sip and put the glass down. "It was horrible," he admitted. "We started out so simply: the quest for free publicity, and then it mushroomed, on and on, finally ending in so much death."

"No one could have predicted such a thing," she whispered.

"And you were supposed to be safely in the van with Seymour!" Richie said. "What's wrong with that jerk? If anything had happened to you—"

"It didn't. And I'm glad I didn't listen to him. If I hadn't been there, a cop might have been killed by that skinny monster."

He shook his head. "Okay. I won't punch Seymour out next time I see him. Which I hope is never."

"Good," she said sincerely.

He took a deep breath. "I wonder if I'll ever stop seeing that sight. The blood, and then the fire." He visibly shuddered.

She gave his shoulder a small supportive rub, then dropped her hand. "Tell me what happened."

He leaned forward, forearms resting on his thighs. "Well, despite what my law enforcement friends were all thinking," he said with a quick glance at her, "I never believed Hanemoto had killed Shig, let alone butchered him. They'd been friends, close friends. Also, beheadings are becoming a big favorite of Mexican drug gangs as a way to strike terror in their enemies. El Grande's little visit with me told me all I needed to know. And the fact that he was crazy enough to go after your sister ... I knew he had to be eliminated."

"Why didn't you tell me any of this?"

"Because it was all feeling—I had no proof of anything, and you and Seymour seemed pretty convinced Hanemoto was the killer. In one way, you were right." He ignored her grimace and sat upright as he continued. "After I left you and Seymour, yesterday, Shay and I went to Kyoto Dreams for dinner and to set up the meeting with Hanemoto. While I talked with Hanemoto, Shay excused himself, and studied the layout of the back of the restaurant. He unlocked one of the windows. Later, when the restaurant was closed and everyone left, around midnight, he snuck inside and waited.

"He knew nothing was supposed to happen until four A.M., but about two-thirty, he heard the front door open. It was El Grande and his men. He sent me a text letting me know both that he was in the restaurant, and that we were right—El Grande had shown up."

"El Grande broke in?" Rebecca asked, surprised.

"I suspect they used Shig's key. For all we know they may still ... still have his body. Anyway, they checked out the place, and thought it was empty. Shay knows how to disappear, believe me."

"I was wondering how they had gotten past the police," Rebecca said. "And, now, it turns out that they snuck inside ahead of all of us. But where was Shay hiding?"

For the first time since he left the restaurant, Richie smiled. "When El Grande entered the restaurant, Shay went into the women's room. He pulled all the doors shut and stood on a toilet seat so they couldn't see his feet. There's something about women's rooms that makes men uneasy. Kind of creeps us out, in fact. We want to get out of them as quickly as possible. I suspect that's why no one checked each stall."

She shook her head at that bit of Too Much Information.

"Anyway, they went back into the storeroom next to Hanemoto's office and waited for the rest of us to arrive. I suspect, the way the restaurant went up in flames so fast, they must have heavily doused it with gasoline while they were waiting. That was the one thing Shay and I hadn't thought of—that El Grande would want to completely destroy the place."

He took a deep breath and then continued. "You probably heard a lot of what was said. El Grande needed to personally take revenge on Bosque's killer because Bosque was family. And he did. Then, when he and his guy were concentrating on setting the fire and, I'm sorry to say, kill me, Shay was able to sneak up behind them and pick them off one by one. Grande's bodyguard got off one shot, but it was wild."

"When I heard those gunshots ..."

"I know," he said, his hand against her cheek. "I'm sorry. Shay put his gun in Hanemoto's guard's hand, making it look like the two groups killed each other. I told your pal, Seymour, that's what happened, while I hid under a table—which was kind of true, come to think of it. Anyway, our biggest problem— before any of this even started—was how we would get Shay out of there without him being seen. We definitely didn't want him to be questioned by the police. But once we heard the SWAT team would be at the scene, Shay got his hands on a uniform, and that problem was solved."

She nodded. "It makes sense. Crazy, but it makes sense ... except for one thing. Why did El Grande show up? How could he have known about the meeting?"

She watched a strange play of emotions on his face. "It seems someone called him with a tip—told him he'd hear a confession and have a chance to take revenge on Bosque's killer."

"But no one knew ..." She stopped talking. No one but her, the FBI, Shay, and Richie. And Shay would never call in such a tip unless told to.

"So, you and Shay," she swallowed hard as the full extent of his plan sunk in, "you two figured out how to get rid of El Grande, one of the most dangerous drug lords in the area."

"Maybe so," he admitted.

Who is this man? "My God! Are you crazy?"

"Don't think of it that way," he said. "Think of it as avenging some friends and making sure that I—and you—are safe from El Grande and his goons. For sure, I would have been next on his list, and you, too, might have been in danger."

She knew he was right. "The fire burned up most of the evidence of what actually happened, so I suspect the surviving gang members won't come after you. And especially not after they hear Seymour's story that all you did was to hide under the table while the two groups killed each other." She couldn't help but smile. "I'm sure he'll love telling that to anyone who'll listen."

"God, but I hate that stuffed shirt," Richie admitted.

"Still, you took a hell of a chance. It was crazy dangerous. So many things could have gone wrong."

"But they didn't. Not this time, at least."

His last words were like a knife to the chest. *Not this time ...* Worry, amazement, and misgivings mixed in a maddening cacophony, even as every iota of her being cheered at what he and Shay had managed to pull off. "Right now," she said, "all I know is that I thank God you survived."

He put his arms around her. "And all I know is I've never seen anything as beautiful as you waiting for me when I got out of that hell hole."

His sweet words made her throat feel thick. As she looked into his eyes, she couldn't help but think of how close she'd come to losing him that night. It was the sort of thing that focused one's mind, that made a person realize what—and who —was truly important. He was far more important to her than she had allowed herself to admit. But she admitted it now to herself and—thinking of the public way she'd kissed him—to everyone who knew her, as a matter of fact.

"What am I going to do with you?" she whispered, scarcely able to speak so much emotion coursed through her.

He drew her closer and kissed her lightly. "I've got an idea."

Her arms went around him as her heart filled with joy and desire. "I thought you were exhausted."

He stretched out on the sofa, shifting so that she lay beside him. Then, to her surprise, he propped himself up and watched her face, her eyes, as he gently ran his hand along her cheek, her neck, her collarbone, down along her side to her hip. There, he stopped for only a moment as he leaned forward and whispered, "Not anymore."

*Find out what happens next in the lives of Rebecca and Richie when the clock strikes **FIVE**...*

Here's the first chapter of FIVE O'CLOCK TWIST:

It was midnight, and San Francisco Homicide Inspector Rebecca Mayfield stood alone on a cold, desolate beach. The biting wind off the Pacific Ocean hit hard. Earlier the fog had rolled in, heavy, thick, and wet. She hugged her black leather jacket tight against her body.

Rebecca and her partner, Bill Sutter, were the current "on-call" team which meant they were the first detectives sent to any suspicious death in the city. Tonight's call from the police dispatcher directed Rebecca to Baker's Beach.

The beach was nearly a mile long, edging what had once been a U.S. Army base, the Presidio of San Francisco. It was now part of the Golden Gate National Recreation Area. She had driven onto its parking lot which was the only area where the street was level with the beach. Past it, the street rose quickly following cliffs that skirted the beach all the way to the Golden Gate Bridge.

The lot's street lamps, blanketed by fog, cast an eerie glow over the deserted surroundings. No squad cars with uniformed police secured the scene. Also absent were the medical examiner's team, the crime scene unit, a photographer, and all the myriad others who always showed up at potential homicides. All was quiet except for the sound of waves against the shore, and the strong, persistent wind.

She couldn't even hear traffic noise, which was particularly unnerving for a city cop.

Rebecca was sure she had been sent to the wrong place. Although she was often the first detective to arrive, the uniforms were always there. This was crazy.

She took out her phone and was about to call the dispatcher when she saw a flashlight. "You from Homicide?" a male voice called. She looked, but could barely make out the figure holding the large bright light directed at her.

"Mayfield." Rebecca identified herself and held up her badge. "You are?" she asked, trying to shield her eyes from the bright light to see at least an outline of the person she was speaking to.

"Officer Garcia. Crime scene's at the far end of the beach. Just walk north. You'll find it."

"Where is everyone?" she asked.

Garcia took a few steps backwards. "The officers are parked at the top of the cliff. There's a pathway down, a shortcut, so they took it. But the fog is even thicker now, so it might be making the rocks we took kind of wet and slick. It's a longer walk to take the beach, but probably safer. They sent me here to tell you and the others the best way to find them. Sorry that you got here before I did. Must have confused you a bit. Anyway, we're all on the same page now. I'm heading out to the entrance to the parking lot. I'll wave the CSI and others in here."

This was just plain weird, Rebecca thought. The beam from the officer's flashlight continued to blind her. She turned her head away from him. "Okay. Guess I walk," she said.

"You can't miss it," the officer called. He was already some distance away, heading towards the street. "Just before the rocks."

Almost the entire beach lay "just before the rocks." No wonder the uniforms had taken a shortcut. Her boots sank into the sand with each step, making the going slow. She had been out here a couple of times at a beach party, times when the evening was warm, when moonlight cast a glow over the water, and stars filled the night sky in a sparkling array. But tonight was different. No light made its way through the fog, and even the lighthouse out on the Farallon Islands might have been extinguished.

The briny smell of the sea was so thick it seemed to attach itself to her skin, hair, and even her lips.

She flicked on her small pocket flashlight. Droplets of fog turned everything in the light's path into a shimmering halo. She had to direct the beam downward simply to see where she was stepping. Something about all this felt "off." She paused. Maybe she should wait for the others and walk out there together with them.

But Officer Garcia had most likely radioed the other uniforms that she was on her way. They would be looking for her. Was she supposed to say she was too "scared" to walk on a beach alone, given her training and the powerful weapon she carried? No way. She'd never live it down. She squared her shoulders and trudged on, her jeans-clad legs taking long, purposeful strides.

While the southern beach area, near the parking lot, was popular on warm, sunny days, especially since nude bathing—typically "San Francisco"—was allowed, the northern portion was a different story. The sandy beach ended at a low-lying wall of rocky outcrops. Climbing over the boulders led to several small, secluded cove-like areas butting up against steep cliffs, and separated one from the other by massive, slippery rocks.

She couldn't help but chuckle to herself as she thought of how her partner, Bill Sutter, was going to react when he was told to walk down a dark, freezing beach at midnight to find the crime scene. He'd swear a blue streak over getting sand in his shoes, and that was just the start of it.

He hated anything that caused him to feel less than absolutely in charge. Sometimes he was fine, but other times, he acted as if he was afraid of his own shadow, let alone the dark. He was often referred to as "Never-Take-a-Chance Bill" because of it.

Richie Amalfi, the man she was currently dating, swore that if she wasn't careful, Sutter was going to get her killed. Richie said she needed a partner who had her back, not one who'd cut and run first chance he got. She thought he was wrong about that, and perhaps, wrong about a lot of things. Including their relationship.

She had given Richie a lot of thought lately; too much thought, in fact. It made her heart heavy to think about him, and all that would never be between them. But she was nothing if not practical, and the practical side of her nature told her it was time to move on.

Yet, trying to put him out of her mind was difficult, if not impossible. In fact, he had phoned her a couple of times as she drove out here tonight. They were working on a case together. Not that she should have been involving him in her homicide investigations, but as usual, he seemed to know the people who had gotten caught up in a murder, and she found his knowledge of them helpful.

She didn't answer his calls. Given the time of night and all that had happened earlier between them, his calls couldn't be anything but personal. For the moment, she needed to concentrate on where she was going and her reason for going there. Not on Richie.

As she continued along the beach, the hill that edged it grew higher and steeper, resulting in a cliff-like edifice that trapped the fog and made it increasingly thick. Now, swirling billows of mist hugged the ground, and the aura of light her flashlight created was so blinding she could scarcely see beyond her hand.

There had been a time when Rebecca enjoyed the heavy San Francisco fog. "Pea soup," the old timers called it. But that was years ago when she first came to the city, and before she had seen an eternity of ugliness on her job that muted the city's charm.

As she continued towards the rocks, the silence bothered her. She should be hearing something from the secured crime scene by now. Instead, the only sounds she heard were the lapping of ocean waves against the shore and the occasional, mournful call of a foghorn.

Up ahead, she could just make out the rocks.

And no crime scene.

The unwanted thought struck that there was never a crime scene out here.

Her breathing quickened, and the skin on her arms prickled.

How could that be? The police dispatcher ...

The dull worry that something was dreadfully wrong turned into a thunderous roar. Every fiber of her being told her to run. She dropped the lit flashlight to the ground, escaping into the fog. Then, instead of heading back down the beach in the direction she came from, she ran as fast as she could in the loose sand towards the cliffs.

As she did, a hail of gunshots went off directed at the light. She heard the sound of metal and glass exploding as her flashlight went out.

She forced herself to keep going as shots flew all around. She hurtled towards the cliffs; only there might she find some kind of shelter. The rapid-fire roar of the fusillade told her that her adversary was using a semi-automatic rifle, a serious killing machine. The shooter was firing blind—even a night scope was useless in the dense mist.

She didn't shoot back, thankful for the shielding fog, and knowing her chance of hitting a shooter she couldn't see was nil.

When she reached the cliff, she all but hugged it, trying to find some boulder, some crevice, anything that might provide shelter. A shot pinged near her and she saw a flash. The shooter must have realized she was searching the cliffs for shelter rather than trying to return to the parking lot.

Finally, she located a spot where a bit of the cliff face curved inward, eroded by the constant pummeling of wind and surf. She hugged the inlet, her back against it, standing as straight and flat as possible. Another hail of bullets, one after the other, cut a swath across the cliff face where she had been standing just seconds earlier. When the shooting stopped, she returned fire, again and again, aiming in the direction of the flash from the firearm.

There were no other cops around, and now she knew there wouldn't be. She'd been set up and directed out here to get her alone. To kill her.

She was scared, more scared than she'd ever been. She didn't want to die.

More shots came her way, and she fired back again and again, even though she recognized that, just that as she had done earlier, her attacker kept moving. She made a mental count of how many bullets she had used, and how few she had left. She knew the way this was going, all the attacker had to do was to wait until she was out of ammunition.

She lay flat on the ground. With both hands on her SIG Sauer, her arms outstretched, she waited for the shooter to move closer. One on one. Whoever saw the other first, she believed, would be the one to live.

Continue with FIVE O'CLOCK TWIST...

ABOUT THE AUTHOR

Joanne Pence was born and raised in northern California. She has been an award-winning, *USA Today* best-selling author of mysteries for many years, but she has also written historical fiction, contemporary romance, romantic suspense, and a fantasy. All of her books are now available as ebooks and in print, and most are also offered in special large print editions and audiobooks. Joanne hopes you'll enjoy her books, which present a variety of times, places, and reading experiences, from mysterious to thrilling, emotional to lightly humorous, as well as powerful tales of times long past.

Visit her at www.joannepence.com and be sure to sign up for Joanne's mailing list to hear about new books.

Contemporary, Historical and Fantasy Novels

Seems Like Old Times

When Lee Reynolds, nationally known television news anchor, returns to the small town where she was born to sell her now-vacant childhood home, little does she expect to find that her first love has moved back to town. Nor does she expect that her feelings for him are still so strong.

Tony Santos had been a major league baseball player, but now finds his days of glory gone. He's gone back home to raise his young son as a single dad.

Both Tony and Lee have changed a lot. Yet, being with him, she finds that in her heart, it seems like old times...

Dangerous Journey

Set in 1978, when Hong Kong was still a British Crown Colony, C.J. Perkins arrives in the maze of the city searching for her brother, who vanished during a Peace Corps assignment. She's chasing the only lead she has—a whisper about something called the White Dragon. The authorities dismiss her questions, the Peace Corps offers regrets instead of answers, and every door she knocks on seems to close in her face.

Her only real option is Darius Kane: adventurer, bounty hunter, and the kind of man who knows how to survive in the shadows between law and crime. C.J. practically shanghais him into the search, forcing an uneasy partnership neither of them wants—but both of them need.

C.J. and Darius follow a trail that takes them through the narrow streets of Hong Kong, the backrooms of San Francisco's Chinatown, and the wild jungles of Borneo as they pursue both her brother and the White Dragon. The closer C.J. gets to them, the more danger she finds herself in—and it's not just danger of losing her life, but also of losing her heart.

Dance with a Gunfighter

Willa Cather Literary Award finalist for Best Historical Novel

Set in the lawless Arizona Territory of the 1870s, Gabriella Devere sets out to avenge her family's murder after a gang of outlaws leaves her with nothing but grief. With no help from the authorities, she rides into outlaw country alone, determined to make the men who destroyed her life answer for their sins.

Jess McLowry left his war-torn Southern home to head West, where he hired out his gun. When he learns what happened to Gabriella's family, and what she plans, he knows a young woman like her will have no chance against the outlaws, and vows to save her the way he couldn't save his own family.

But the price of vengeance is high and Gabriella's willingness to sacrifice everything ultimately leads to the book's deadly and startling conclusion.

The Ghost of Squire House

For decades, the home built by reclusive artist, Paul Squire, has stood empty on a windswept cliff overlooking the ocean. Those who attempted to live in the home soon fled in terror. Jennifer Barrett knows nothing of the history of the house she inherited. All she knows is she's glad for the chance to make a new life for herself.

A compelling, prickly ghost with a tortured, guilt-ridden past, and a lonely heroine determined to start fresh, find themselves in a battle of wills and emotion in this ghostly fantasy of love, time, and chance.

The Dragon's Lady

Turn-of-the-century San Francisco comes to life in this romance of star-crossed lovers whose love is forbidden by both society and the laws of the time.

Ruth Greer, wealthy daughter of a shipping magnate, finds a young boy who has run away from his home in Chinatown—an area of gambling parlors, opium dens, and sing-song girls, as well as families trying to eke out a living. It is also home to the infamous and deadly "hatchet men" of Chinese lore.

There, Ruth meets Li Han-lin, a handsome, enigmatic leader of one such tong. The two are from completely different worlds, and when both worlds are shattered by the Great Earthquake and Fire of 1906 that destroyed most of San Francisco, they face their ultimate test.

The Donnelly Cabin Inn Series

Three half-sisters inherit a remote cabin, but there's just one problem with it. It's haunted.

IF I LOVED YOU
THIS CAN'T BE LOVE
SENTIMENTAL JOURNEY
A CERTAIN SMILE
TIME AFTER TIME

The Rebecca Mayfield Mysteries

Rebecca is a by-the-book detective, who walks the straight and narrow in her work, and in her life. Richie, on the other hand, is not at all by-the-book. But opposites can and do attract, and there are few mystery two-somes quite as opposite as Rebecca and Richie.

ONE O'CLOCK HUSTLE – North American Book Award winner in Mystery
TWO O'CLOCK HEIST
THREE O'CLOCK SÉANCE
FOUR O'CLOCK SIZZLE
FIVE O'CLOCK TWIST
SIX O'CLOCK SILENCE
SEVEN O'CLOCK TARGET
EIGHT O'CLOCK SPLIT
NINE O'CLOCK RETREAT
Plus a Christmas Novella: The Thirteenth Santa

The Cook and Inspector Mysteries

Gourmet cook Angie Amalfi and San Francisco Homicide Inspector Paavo Smith face crime and calories in this now complete mystery series:
DEATH ON A SILVER PLATTER
A QUICHE BEFORE DYING
THE MARINARA MURDERS
CLOSE ENCOUNTERS OF THE DEADLY KIND
DEATH BY DEVIL'S FOOD

BLIND DATE'S BITTER END
THE TAVERNA AFFAIR
THE MUSIC BOX MYSTERY
TRUFFLES TO DIE FOR
COOKING SPIRITS
ADD A PINCH OF MURDER
SALSA AND SECRETS
DEADLY EVER AFTER